G. Curzon

Delamere

Vol. II

G. Curzon

Delamere
Vol. II

ISBN/EAN: 9783337067519

Printed in Europe, USA, Canada, Australia, Japan

Cover: Foto ©Andreas Hilbeck / pixelio.de

More available books at **www.hansebooks.com**

DELAMERE.

A Novel.

BY

G. CURZON,

AUTHOR OF "THE VIOLINIST OF THE QUARTIER LATIN."

IN THREE VOLUMES.
VOL. II.

LONDON:

SAMPSON LOW, MARSTON, SEARLE & RIVINGTON,

CROWN BUILDINGS, 188, FLEET STREET.

1886.

DELAMERE.

CHAPTER I.

An hour passed, and Teresa and Bernard were still together in the gardens, but Fleurette was no longer the subject of discussion. Having set matters in train for getting the child into his power, Bernard was too wise to waste an unnecessary word upon her. Teresa herself was now his theme, and he was in a very complimentary humour; but the day was too cold and raw for much love-making, and a heavy shower of sleet, mingled with snow, reconciled the Italian girl to

return to her lodgings, on the promise
that Bernard would call for her in the
evening, and escort her to the 'Alhambra.
She took a cab at the gate, as it was
wet underfoot; but Bernard refused the
vacant seat beside her, although his way
lay in the same direction as hers. He
was cold, he said, from loitering about so
long, and a smart walk would do him
good.

Relieved at having got rid of Teresa,
he set off at a brisk pace to Spiers and
Pond's, where a good luncheon and sundry
glasses of sherry soothed his feelings, and
inclined him to take a more amicable
view of things in general. He took a
hansom afterwards to Bond Street, and
alighted at a stationer's. His sister,
Mrs. de Ruthvyn, wanted some of her
cards in a hurry, he told one of the
young men. Fifty would do, but they

should be left at 15, Jermyn Street, by five o'clock at the latest.

Upon being assured that the order would receive prompt attention, Bernard reseated himself in the hansom and drove to the Victoria Station, where he ascertained that the train in communication with the steamer left at eleven in the morning. He inquired the price of a second-class ticket to Paris, and made a very close calculation of what Teresa would be likely to spend at the Hotel de Lille et d'Albion for two or three days. On his way home, he turned into the Strand, and at a cheap jeweller's in that crowded thoroughfare expended a sovereign on a pair of earrings.

The rapture with which the Italian girl received them a couple of hours later would have delighted a more warm-hearted lover, but Bernard checked her ardour.

She could go into ecstasies by-and-by about them, he told her, but he begged her not to make a commotion while he was in the house. Teresa, however, insisted upon wearing her new finery at the theatre, and Bernard was left in a small room full of mysterious boxes and packing-cases over Madame Bertrand's millinery rooms, while she fastened the trinkets in her ears, and put the finishing touches to her toilet. Within ten minutes she reappeared, and, after a final survey of herself in the dingy mirror at the end of the room, they started together for Leicester Square.

It was an evening long to be remembered by Teresa. The burlesque was not very refined, but she was not over-fastidious, and she was passionately fond of any kind of dramatic representation. After the performance, she and Bernard

went to Gatti's, where they had a supper-
table to themselves, in a quiet corner,
and there he transferred five sovereigns
from his purse to hers ; also his sister's
visiting-cards, which had duly reached his
lodgings that afternoon. On his way to
Oxford Street, he told her that he had
altered his plans, and that he wished her
to postpone her departure for another day,
in order to give him time to ascertain
beyond doubt that Fleurette was in Paris.
He intended to start for Delamere the
following morning, to find out the precise
address of the child ; and if on inquiry he
found that she was not in the convent,
he would telegraph to her to remain in
London. If, on the other hand, he did
not telegraph, she was to pursue her
journey as directed.

Bernard did not go home to his lodgings
after he parted with Teresa. He turned

into Piccadilly, and, meeting some of his
boon companions, played billiards with
them at his club until the small hours.
It was not a good preparation for his
journey, and he woke the next morning
with a headache ; but he was in a reckless,
irritable humour, and was impatient to
be off to Delamere. He foresaw that he
would have some unpleasantness with
Evelyn, and, to nerve himself for it,
consumed a good deal of brandy on the
road. He was consequently in a very
excitable condition when the train arrived
at Stockford, and, on discovering that no
vehicle awaited him from Delamere, was
inclined to quarrel with the porters, the
guard, and all the officials with whom
he came in contact. He waited twenty
minutes at the station, to see if the
brougham would arrive, and then engaged
a fly to drive him the fourteen miles that

intervened between the station and the park.

While Bernard was jolting in the hired carriage to Delamere, Evelyn and her solicitor were closeted together in the library of the castle, discussing a subject which had weighed upon her mind during the last two years. The interview was a painful one to her, although she had been very eager for it; but, as she was bent upon sifting the mystery of Fleurette's parentage, she was resolved to give no half-confidences to the man on whom she was relying for assistance.

Mr. Hilton was very much puzzled at first. It flashed upon him, during the early portion of the interview, that Evelyn was astray in her head—he could account in no other way for her feverish anxiety to dispossess her son of his property; but when he read the letter which she handed

him, and which she said was a copy of
the one she destroyed, he began to see
things more clearly. He remembered a
day, about three weeks or a month before
Randolph's death, when he came by appointment to see him, and was alone
with him for nearly an hour. He reminded Evelyn of it now, and told her
that Randolph had on that occasion
talked of making a new will, and was
very much agitated. His mind was quite
disordered at the time, and, though he
was so full of making the will when Mr.
Hilton arrived, it seemed to pass out of
his thoughts ten minutes afterwards.
From that day to this, he, Mr. Hilton,
had heard nothing of such a document.
Randolph's allusion to the marriage certificate seemed of greater significance in
his eyes, and he questioned Evelyn very
closely upon her reasons for thinking that

Fleurette was the legitimate child of Philip de Ruthvyn. Evelyn relieved him by mentioning that before destroying the letter she had made a search through her husband's papers, and had found neither a will nor a certificate. The lawyer's stolid countenance brightened up at this news. "What matter about Randolph's letter?" he exclaimed. It was mere waste paper. It was not worth a rush unless corroborated by other proofs. Raymond's worst enemies could make nothing of so feeble a case. Mr. Hilton endeavoured to reassure Evelyn, but he did not find the task an easy one. He affected to treat the matter as beneath consideration. Randolph's mind was weak, in his opinion, for many weeks before his death, and it was absurd to attach importance to either his writings or his words.

After some more discussion, he followed

Evelyn upstairs, and spent an hour with her in searching every drawer and desk for the missing papers. She pointed out the oaken cabinet referred to in the letter, and they both examined it in vain. Mr. Hilton was not sorry when the lunch-bell put an end to the fruitless search, and, having heard all that Evelyn had to say about Fleurette, he took his leave, promising to set inquiries on foot, and to let her know from time to time the result of his investigations.

CHAPTER II.

THE cold winds of March have been followed by the genial showers of April, and that capricious month has, in its turn, been replaced by the warm sunshine of May. Spring is no longer in its crude stage of nipping easterly wind, but is fast merging into summer. It is the season of hope and expectancy, and each day adds to the beauty of the newly awakened earth. The air teems with fragrance and melody; starry primroses and wild hyacinths carpet the woods; and the birds sing their most joyous songs, as if partaking in the universal gladness of nature.

On one of these lovely May mornings, Captain Stamer is sauntering in the direction of the river that skirts the Broomhill demesne. He has just come from Fred Brandreth's smoking-den, where he has selected a light rod and some fine tackle, and is looking forward to two or three hours' lazy enjoyment, the rest of the party having started in the waggonette for a long drive. There is no perceptible change in his appearance since he crossed to Ostend with Bernard Waldstein. The fair though bronzed face, the light brown hair and moustache, and the clearly cut features, are unaltered. He is still strikingly handsome, and, though sad and stern-looking in repose, his face lights up when animated, and is irresistibly fascinating as of old. Captain Stamer has a *penchant* for the river. He loves the sheltered nooks beneath the overhanging

willows, and he spends many hours upon
its banks. On the other side stretch the
woods and park of Delamere, and in many
an hour of seeming indolence his thoughts
revert to Evelyn.

When journeying from London to
Daleshire three weeks ago, he persuaded
himself that he was not in love with her.
He had got over that bygone infatuation,
and it was from mere curiosity that he
wished to see her again. He had made
an attempt to renew his intimacy with
her last year, but before he arrived at
Broomhill she had left the neighbourhood
for Scotland. He soothed his wounded
vanity, however, on that occasion with
the thought that her sudden journey was
caused by her mother's illness, and not
by a wish to avoid him, and he resolved
to try his chance again. It was many
years since he and Evelyn had met, and

she had probably so changed and fallen off in her appearance that a look would cure him.

It was in church, a few Sundays ago, that Donald first saw his cousin after the long lapse of years, and almost before he saw her he felt that her influence over him was unchanged. It is not easy to throw off an infatuation; and even if Evelyn had lost her beauty, it is probable that Donald would not have perceived it. Her plainness would have been more alluring to him than the faultlessness of any other woman; but if he had never been infatuated by her, if she had not been the ruling idea of his mind for many years past, if he saw her three weeks ago for the first time and as a total stranger, he could not fail to have admired her. He would have been attracted by the tall, graceful figure; he would have been fascinated by the pale face, with the sweet, sad mouth and the dark, expressive eyes. There were no lines on the smooth white brow, no silver threads in the dark brown hair, and her figure was lithe and slender as when he knew her as a girl at Monkhurst.

The second Sunday, he noticed a pretty child in the same pew with Evelyn. It was Fleurette, who no longer wore black, but was dressed in a dark-brown velvet pelisse, trimmed with silver fox, and cap to match. Knowing that Evelyn had no daughter, he could not think who the golden-haired child was, and she was equally puzzled about him. Fleurette knew that he came to church with the Brandreths, and wondered why he never came to Delamere with them. Fred was constantly at the park; Marian, a gushing young lady, with pale blue eyes and a lisp, came often to afternoon tea; even old Mrs. Brandreth would come now and then, and have a confidential talk with Evelyn; but the stranger never appeared. Fleurette felt a great interest in him. He had such a nice, kind face, she thought, and his eyes wandered so often in the direction of their pew. Donald knew that she was inclined to be friendly to him, and was quite ready to be amicable in return. The fact that she was connected with Evelyn gave him an additional charm in his eyes, and he believed that she could be the means of breaking down the reserve that existed between him and his cousin, if he could only meet her and have an opportunity of talking to her; but she was as invisible as Evelyn herself. He never saw them except on Sundays, and they either remained in church after the others, or vanished before he had time to overtake them. On inquiry, he heard from the Brandreths that she was the orphan daughter of Arthur de Ruthvyn, and that she was being brought up under Evelyn's care at Delamere. She was at school from Monday to Saturday, which accounted for his seeing her so seldom.

Captain Stamer had called at the park the day after his arrival, but Evelyn was not at home, and he had to content himself with the formality of leaving a card. From that day to the present he has spent many hours on the river-side, casting eager glances at the opposite woods, and vainly watching for a glimpse of the figure which has still such power to charm him. Will they ever meet and speak to each other again as in the days of old, or is she determined to ignore his very existence?

Donald feels unusually dejected this bright May morning. He has not been successful in his sport. There has been too much sun for the fish to bite, and, though he has idled away a couple of hours, he has only caught a few small perch. The loss of time does not trouble him much, as he came to this quiet spot for the purpose of thinking of Evelyn. The river in front divides him from her. He has only to get into a boat, and he will be beside her in ten minutes. But he is not in visiting costume; besides, she has so persistently avoided him, that she may think it effrontery if he calls so soon again.

He was reflecting on the advisability of going back to Broomhill, changing his dress, and taking a stroll in the direction of the park gate, in the hopes of meeting her, when he was attracted by voices on the opposite bank, and, looking in the direction of the sound, he perceived some small figures among the trees on the Delamere side of the river. They were at too great a distance for him to recognize them, and they were concealed every now and then by the trees, but he had little doubt they were Fleurette and Evelyn's youngest boy. Donald walked along the little footpath by the river-side until he came directly opposite them. The river was narrower here, and he could distinguish them better. It was Fleurette, beyond a doubt. She wore a holland dress, and her face was partly concealed by a wide straw hat; but he knew her by the fair hair, which hung below her waist, and, acting on the impulse of the moment, he sprang into a little boat that was moored alongside the bank, and paddled over to the opposite side. Fleurette would not be very stand-off with him, he expected. He would get into conversation with her without much difficulty, and she would tell him what Evelyn did with herself, and where she spent her afternoons.

CHAPTER III.

It is a week since Donald crossed the river and made Fleurette's acquaintance. It is just such another bright May day, and the little girl, who has not been banished to a convent school in Paris, but thinks it quite a sufficient grievance to be located at Allerton House, Didscombe, for the greater part of each week, is seated on a rustic stile, and looks very pretty and picturesque. These are the Easter holidays, and she is doing her best to forget that there is such a place as Allerton House. She has put lessons out of her head, and is as happy as a queen.

A week of the vacation is passed, but she has a fortnight before her, and Raymond is coming home to-morrow.

Meantime, she has not been lonely. Standing close beside her, with his arms leaning on the low wall of the stile, and talking to her as familiarly as if they were old friends, is Donald Stamer. He has made a staunch friend of Fleurette since the first day of his acquaintance with her, as he had the good fortune on that occasion to rescue her favourite Blenheim spaniel from the clutches of a bull terrier of Fred Brandreth's, and she has looked upon him as a benefactor to humanity ever since. She was at Broomhill to-day, with a note from Evelyn to Mrs. Brandreth, and Donald has come back with her through the fields as far as the stile, lest the Blenheim should be attacked by any stray dog. She is holding the animal in her arms, and, while sitting on the stile to rest, is showing Donald a sore spot on his paw, which, she insists, is the result of the fight with the terrier.

" Quiet, Spot, quiet!" she says, addressing the animal, who cocks his ears, and shows a desire to jump out of her arms.

There is a succession of sharp yelps. Fleurette looks round, and a glossy King Charles springs up the far side of the stile, knocks the Blenheim out of her lap, and rolls head over heels with him in the grass.

"Naughty Tiny! how did you manage to break loose?" says Fleurette, addressing the new-comer. "Down, sir, down! You will hurt Spot's leg."

"Let them tumble about; they won't hurt each other, you may rest assured.

Is this the quarrelsome little animal that you are afraid to bring to Broomhill with you?" continued Donald, pointing with his stick to the King Charles.

"Yes," answered Fleurette; "he is naughty sometimes, and Fred has so many dogs that he would be sure to get into mischief with some of them. He is quite different from Spot, who would never fight unless he was attacked." As Fleurette spoke, she stooped and caressed her favourite.

"You are very partial to Spot, Fleurette. Tiny is the prettier of the two. He is a little beauty, and a complete thoroughbred."

"But he is not half so affectionate as Spot. He does not love me one bit. The only person he cares for is Uncle Bernard. Perhaps that is natural, as he belonged to him first, and he had all the trouble of training him for me."

"I used to know Bernard Waldstein," said Donald. "Where is he now?"

"He was here three weeks ago for a couple of days, but I don't know where he is now," said Fleurette, gravely. "I very much fear that he and Aunt Evelyn have had a falling out," she continued, looking seriously at Donald.

"It must be a terrible falling out, to judge by your sober looks, Fleurette," said Donald, with a smile.

"It was all because the brougham did not meet him at the railway station; but it was the coachman's fault, for Aunt Evelyn told him to set off in time. Bernard had to take a fly, and I believe he insisted on driving himself, and had an upset. He was in a great rage when he arrived at the castle, and said he was very much hurt. Clarice told me that he was very rude to Aunt Evelyn next day, and that he was quarrelling with her about me. I have often wondered what it was about."

Donald paid little heed to the child's talk, though his eyes were fixed intently upon her. He was thinking how pretty she was, and what joy or sorrow she would cause in the future to some who were probably unconscious of her existence as yet. Would she become heartless and deceitful as the years rolled by? Would she bring desolation to the lives of others, and be as haughtily indifferent to their suffering as Evelyn had been to his? How charming she was now, in the freshness of her innocent childhood! But she must inevitably change. She must alter, body, mind, and spirit, for the better or worse, and be a totally different being in a few years.

"What are you thinking of?" said

Fleurette, looking at her companion with a bright smile, and wondering at his unusual silence.

If she had been a few years younger, Donald would have told her that his thoughts were of herself; but she was old enough to understand, and he did not wish to be the first to make her self-conscious.

"I am thinking that while you and I are talking about Bernard, the dogs are having a fine time with old Mrs. Grisney's chickens down in the hollow. See how they are chasing them!"

The colour rose to Fleurette's cheeks, and a look of alarm spread over her face at this news. "They are only a week old; they will be killed to a certainty," she said, looking hastily in the direction of the cottage. Then, springing to her feet, and without waiting for Donald to assist her, she jumped off the stile and ran down the hollow with the agility of a fawn, her hat falling off, and her long hair waving in the wind.

Donald followed more leisurely, and, before he reached the cottage, met her returning with the dogs in her arms.

"I just stopped them in time," she said, panting for breath, and with a bright colour in her cheeks from the exercise. "Tiny was frightening a poor little chicken to death. It was all in a flutter; I could see its little heart beating : and Spot was nearly as bad. Luckily, the wee chickens were at the back of the cottage in the barn. Mrs. Grisney has two clutches, you know; one came out this spring, and the other last, and Fred's big mastiff has killed several of them already. Will you carry Tiny for me?" continued she, handing Donald the King

Charles. "I have cleaned his paws, so
he won't soil you. We had better keep
good hold of them until we get well
away from the chickens."

Donald took hold of the dog reluctantly,
and they continued their way, while
Fleurette gave him a description of Mrs.
Grisney's cottage and all her belongings,
in which he seemed to be deeply interested. A couple of hundred yards
further they reached a small gate on the
outskirts of the Delamere grounds, leading into a wood, and Donald let go the
struggling spaniel.

"We may as well let them down here.
They are too far from the chickens to
think of them any more, and you can get
safely home by yourself from this. I will
bid you good-bye now."

"You must come a little further," said
Fleurette, loosening her hold of Spot and

placing both her hands round Captain
Stamer's arm. "I want to show you my
house. Charlie and Raymond and I have
houses in the wood. We pay each other
visits, and mine is much the prettiest. I
will give you a bunch of violets and
primroses if you come," said she, coax-
ingly.

"You will have a real house of your
own some of these days, little one, and
then I will be sure to come and see you;
but I don't like trespassing."

"Trespassing, indeed!" answered
Fleurette, ironically. "How can you say
you are trespassing when I invite you to
come? This place is all Raymond's, and
whatever is his is mine."

"You are a droll child, Fleurette, and
you always manage to have your own
way," said Donald, laughing, as he walked
beside her into the tangled pathways of

the wood. What do you mean by saying that whatever is Raymond's is yours. Perhaps he won't agree to it?"

"Yes, he will. He and I are to live here together by-and-by, and we are to be as rich and as happy as a prince and a princess in a fairy castle. He never does anything without consulting me, and we are awfully fond of each other."

"I suppose you will be marrying this little sweetheart of yours by-and-by?" said Donald.

"Oh dear, no; we shall not think of marrying. We shall be much happier unmarried. People are always wicked and unhappy when they marry. In the story I was reading last week, the wife used some evil enchantment, and made her husband half marble, and then beat him unmercifully. His cries could be heard a long way off."

"But you would not think of treating Raymond in that way, surely?" said Donald, laughing at her earnestness. "I have no doubt you would use enchantments, for I verily believe you are a little witch; but you would not be so cruel as to beat any one?"

"No, of course not," said Fleurette, laughing at the ridiculous idea. "Whether I marry Raymond or not, I shall always love him quite as much as if he were my own brother. I am very fond of Charlie, too; but I have more fun with Raymond."

"I knew a boy and girl a long time ago, and they were quite as fond of each other as you and Raymond are now," said Donald, in a low tone of voice.

"Tell me about them; do, please," said Fleurette, eagerly. "I like listening to stories better than reading them, and true stories best of all. Did they love each other very much ? "

" Yes, very much ; they were cousins, too, just as you and Raymond are, and spent their holidays in the same house. They became fonder of each other as they grew older ; and then, when the girl was seventeen, and the boy a grown-up man—— "

" Go on," said Fleurette, impatiently, seeing that her companion had suddenly paused in his narrative. " What happened when the girl was seventeen ? Something unhappy, I am sure."

" I almost forget the end of the story. I only remember that it had not a happy ending."

Donald was looking straight in front of him, and his voice had a strange tremor in it. He was conscious of a suffocating feeling ; he knew that his heart was beating painfully, and that a tall, slender, black-robed figure was advancing through the trees to meet him. In another moment he and Evelyn were shaking hands, each making a desperate attempt to appear unconcerned.

Fleurette came to the rescue, but in a very awkward fashion. "Captain Stamer was telling me such a nice story as you came up, Aunt Evelyn. He had just come to the interesting part. Won't you make him go on with it?"

"Another time, Fleurette," said Donald, frowning at her impatiently, and dreading that she would enter into the details of the story. "I told you that I had forgotten the end. I will look it up when I go back to Broomhill, and will be able to tell it to you when next we meet."

"But you said it was all true," insisted Fleurette. "Why should you want to go to Broomhill to remember it if it is true? You said you knew them yourself, and something happened when the girl was seventeen."

"You must not tease, dear," said Evelyn. "Run home and change your frock; you are all over mud, and look most untidy."

Fleurette scampered on in front with the dogs, having first explained that the condition of her frock was entirely owing to the raid upon Mrs. Grisney's chickens.

"I have often been wondering that we did not meet, Donald," said Evelyn, turning back and walking towards the castle with her cousin. She had recovered her composure, the vivid colour had faded from her cheeks, and her complexion looked white as a lily in contrast to her sombre attire. "Do you make a long stay at Broomhill?" she continued.

"Probably a fortnight, but I am not quite certain. You know, I have been three weeks here already."

"And yet this is your first visit to Delamere. I ought to scold you for being so unfriendly," said Evelyn.

"You got my card, surely?" interrupted Donald. "I called the day after I came here, but the servant said you were out."

"I saw your formal little piece of pasteboard; but why did you not come again? I was beginning to think that you had left the neighbourhood, as I never chanced to meet you."

"You know very well that I would have come again and again had I dared," said Donald, with suppressed emotion, as he tried to read the expression of Evelyn's eyes; but she was looking straight before her, and there was nothing to tell of the

wild excitement that was tingling through
her veins. "My only object in coming
to this neighbourhood was to be near
you. I was only waiting for you to give
me a little encouragement."

"I never give any one encouragement,"
answered Evelyn, haughtily. "I should
have been very pleased to see you; but
pray do not imagine that I mean anything else."

After this rebuff, Donald had recourse
to commonplace subjects. He expatiated
on the beauty of the wood; he asked
after Raymond and Charlie; he discussed
Kate's approaching marriage with Fred;
and Evelyn made no more sarcastic re-
joinders, and all constraint seemed at an
end between them.

It was happiness to be beside her, to
listen to her voice, to watch the movements of her figure, to take her hand in

his as he assisted her over a fallen branch or guided her through the tangled mazes of the wood; and, as if to compensate for the rebuff, she looked at him more kindly. There was no longer any haughtiness in her lustrous eyes, but an expression that filled him with the wild desire to tell her, at all cost, that he idolized her still.

Donald, however, set a watch upon his lips. Some future time he might venture to tell her that his feelings for her were unchanged, but it would be premature at present. To act on a rash impulse would be to banish himself from her presence, and he was resolved not to risk it.

"I don't believe you have ever seen Raymond; at least, not since he was quite a little child," said Evelyn. "He and Fleurette are very much of an age, and are great friends. We expect him home for the holidays to-morrow, and you must dine with us the next day. I shall get the Brandreths to come also, and we shall have a social gathering. I never give ceremonious parties now."

Donald accepted the invitation, and did not venture to say how much he would prefer that the Brandreths were not included. He dared not suggest a *tête-à-tête* repast, though he longed for even one hour of her undivided society, and he knew she could manage it if she wished. She was so very charming, but so very cold. She had such a wonderful facility for concealing her feelings—if, indeed, she ever felt. Did she ever think of the past? Did any spark of passion still linger within her? He believed, in spite of her seeming indifference, that she loved him ; but would she continue to be uncompromisingly stern to herself and him ? Was she going to set up the same barrier of reserve between them now as in past days ?

These thoughts flashed through Donald's mind, as he emerged from the wood with Evelyn, and entered one of the avenues leading direct to the castle. How short the walk had seemed! how odiously near the moment of parting!

To defer it for even a little while, he offered to wait while she wrote her note of invitation to Mrs. Brandreth. It would save sending a messenger, he suggested, and he was going back direct; but Evelyn did not take the hint. She would send it in the course of the afternoon, but would not detain him now; and then Fleurette ran back to shake hands with him, and there was nothing left for him but to bid them both a reluctant adieu.

CHAPTER IV.

DONALD was in a sanguine humour after his unexpected meeting with Evelyn, and was inclined to believe that fickle fortune was at length about to favour him. He was almost angry with himself that through want of courage he had forfeited so much of her society, and that he had been so easily damped by her apparent coldness when he first arrived at Broom-hill. All misunderstandings were happily at an end, and a bright vista of happiness opened before him.

He built many castles in the air, as he

walked back through the park, but a
disappointment was in store for him a
few evenings later which he scarcely
expected. The dinner-party at Delamere
was a failure as far as he was concerned.
Old Mrs. Brandreth accepted the invitation, the weather being so mild, and
monopolized much of Evelyn's attention.
The other guests were Mr. Brandreth,
senior—a vigorous, florid-faced county
squire, several years younger looking than
his wife; Fred and Marian Brandreth;
Sir Charles Haughton, a sporting young
baronet of a jovial disposition, who had
come to stay at Broomhill about ten days
before; and Mr. Hurst, the vicar, and his
wife. Donald had not expected that
Evelyn could give him much of her
society, but he had counted on something
more acceptable to his vanity than mere
friendly indifference. Much can be told

in a word or a glance, and she could
have made him supremely happy had she
wished; but she gave him neither glances
nor words different from those she bestowed on her other guests. She had
such a talent for dissimulation that he
did not doubt her indifference was
feigned; but why had she looked so
provokingly happy, and why had she
been so unnecessary civil to that snob,
Sir Charles Haughton?

. As days passed, Donald perceived that
he need not fear a rival in the young
baronet. Evelyn's civilities to him ceased
the night of the dinner-party, and she
resolutely refused his entreaties to join in
the riding-parties and boating-excursions
which he and Fred Brandreth had been
planning. Donald contrived to absent
himself from most of these parties also.
He knew where to find his cousin on

such occasions, and in this delicious spring weather she allowed him to roam with her through the picturesque glades of Delamere, and to forget the disagreeable impressions of his first evening at the castle. Donald was not inclined to find fault with Evelyn for her love of solitude, and, so long as he was not banished from her presence himself, he was pleased that she choose to live the life of a recluse.

By some mutual understanding, they both ignored the past; yet Evelyn felt sometimes tempted to show Donald the letter which was the means of breaking their engagement, and which she has known for many years past to be a forgery. She has never shown it to mortal yet. In the days when she believed it to be genuine, she was too proud to confide her sorrow to any one. She

would not allow even Kate Penthony to
suspect that she had been subjected to
such a humiliation, and since she has
known it to be a forgery, she has equally
hesitated to show it, knowing that it
must be the work of some near relative.
Now, however, she would like to take it
from its hiding-place, and exculpate herself for ever in Donald's eyes by placing
it in his hands. She is not wholly content at believing in him. She wishes
him equally to believe in her. She
wishes him to know all the extenuating
circumstances which led her to break her
faith with him, and the bondage of silence
upon topics that most interest them
which she ruthlessly imposes upon herself is at times intolerable. She solaces
herself with the thought that Donald
loves her, in spite of her supposed false-
ness, and that all such perilous explana-

tions as she longs but dreads to give are, after all, unnecessary.

So they continue to spend blissful hours together, lovers in heart, but masking their feelings under the guise of friendship, each dreading by word or look to bring such meetings to an end. The guise of mere friendship is a still greater effort for Donald to assume. He finds the perpetual restraint almost galling, and he longs to give utterance to the hot, impetuous words that are trembling upon his lips, but which, once spoken, may lead to his banishment. He sometimes forgets all the years that have intervened, and thinks that he is with Evelyn again, as in the brief period of their engagement, when she had no need to shrink from him. He would give worlds for that time to return. Will she ever unbend? Will she ever be anything but ice to his fire? There is a light in her smile and a softness in her eyes that buoys up his hopes. He can scarcely call her cold, when her glance rests on him so tenderly; but she has a languid way of turning aside his homage which gives her a nonchalance and a serenity almost as impossible to overcome as coldness.

It may have been to test her indifference that he talked to her one morning of the likelihood of his regiment being ordered on active service. There was a prospect of an expedition to Ashantee, and he was very glad of it, he said. He was heartily tired of an inactive life, and would volunteer rather than lose the chance of a stirring campaign. However surprised Evelyn may have been at this news, she betrayed no emotion. She discussed Donald's professional prospects with much interest and a good deal more *sang-froid* than he expected, and seemed quite anxious that he should have an opportunity of distinguishing himself.

CHAPTER V.

About three weeks after the dinner-party at Delamere, Evelyn left the castle for a ramble in the wood, followed by Fleurette's favourite spaniel. She crossed the park by one of its least-frequented paths, and entered a lonely glen, deep in the heart of the woodland solitude. The river, scarcely wider than a mountain stream, gurgled noisily through its midst, leaping over the rocks and boulders that impeded its course, and moistening with spray the luxurious growth of ferns and wild flowers upon its borders. The vivid sunshine scarcely penetrated the dense canopy of foliage overhead, and no sound disturbed the stillness, save the rush of the water, the occasional flutter of a rabbit among the ferns, or the sweet notes of the blackbirds and thrushes. It was a favourite retreat of Evelyn's, whenever she felt out of sorts and wished to be secure from intrusion, and she was very much depressed to-day. The news of the approaching war, which had become something more than a mere rumour within the last week, affected her more than she cared to admit, and there were other affairs weighing upon her in which Donald Stamer was in no way connected.

She had received that morning a letter from her solicitor, telling her that he had very important news to communicate with reference to the marriage of the late Philip de Ruthvyn. Mr. Hilton, after alluding to some other business matters, wound up by saying that he was detained in London for a few days, but that he would be at Delamere early the following week. This letter had an agitating effect upon Evelyn. She inferred at a glance that the lawyer had found her surmises to be correct, and had discovered some conclusive evidence of Fleurette's parentage. His next step, no doubt, would be to advise the transfer of the property to the lawful owner, and she must tell Raymond the whole truth without more delay. Better that he should know the facts of the case now than a few years hence, she thought, with a sigh, as she tried to reconcile herself to the exceeding bitterness of the situation. She had done her utmost to aid her husband in his feeble efforts to do right, but she was not blind to the fact that in so doing she had inflicted upon herself a martyrdom.

In carrying out his dying wishes, she had brought misfortune upon her favourite son, and her heart clung all the more fondly to him for that reason. He was the one rival whom Captain Stamer had need to fear. His image rose perpetually before Evelyn, looking at her with mournful earnestness, and disputing the possession of her affections. He was already the victim of his father's evil conduct, and she vowed, with passionate tears, that he should never suffer through her. For his sake, if for nothing else, she would keep to the straight and thorny road. She would trample upon her love for her cousin. She would erase his memory from her heart rather than bring more sorrow and humiliation upon Raymond. Such thoughts were passing through Evelyn's mind, as she crossed the little bridge that spanned the river, and seated herself upon a stone, half buried in ferns. She knew the contents of Mr. Hilton's letter by heart, but she took it out of her pocket and read it again in the quiet stillness of the wood, sighing impatiently at the delay which must ensue before she can know the full meaning of its contents. " Would it be possible to go to London, see Mr. Hilton at his hotel, and thus end this suspense ? " she thinks, as she opens her pocket-book to write down his address, fearing the letter may go astray. She enters it mechanically, but her eyes are riveted on another entry upon the same page, and her thoughts revert to another and scarcely less-harassing subject. She is suddenly reminded that Donald's stay at Broomhill is fast drawing to a close, and that when he leaves Daleshire he is to start for the seat of war.

Would it not be unkind to leave him

when they must perforce part so soon;
when he had already suffered so much at
her hands, and would so keenly feel the
fresh cruelty? He had loved her all his
life long, and it would be inhuman to
desert him now. For the moment Raymond faded into oblivion, and Donald
Stamer usurped every thought of her
mind. She shuddered as she pictured to
herself, in horrible and vivid colouring,
what might befall him on those far-off
African marshes a few weeks hence, and
a sickening sensation crept over her.

Life was looking very dreary to Evelyn
this lovely June morning, while the golden
sunshine flickered through the trees and
the throats of the feathered songsters
were swelling with joyous melody. The
genial sunshine and the flowery-scented
air were powerless to cheer her. They
could not chase the gloom of sorrow from

her heart, nor free her from the cares and anxieties that weighed upon her. Evelyn seldom gave way to emotion. She had such complete mastery over herself, that few had ever seen her weep; but the tears gathered in her eyes to-day, and dropped upon the open letter in her lap. She was so absorbed that she did not hear a well-known footstep coming near her through the fern and underwood, and she started, on looking up, to find Donald Stamer at her side.

"I have been looking for you everywhere, and should never have found you had I not espied Spot through the trees," said Captain Stamer, gaily, his handsome face radiant with delight, and his pulses throbbing at finding himself face to face with his cousin. "But something has grieved you; you look distressed. What is the matter?" he continued, his joyous tone changing to one of alarm, as he noticed Evelyn's tear-stained eyes.

"You cannot help me, Donald, I fear. I have had disagreeable news, that is all," said Evelyn, in an unsteady voice, turning away her head to escape her cousin's earnest questioning gaze; but his unexpected presence had unnerved her afresh, and she found it impossible to recover her composure.

"Evelyn dearest, what has vexed you?" cried Donald. The thought flashing upon him that her tears were caused by his approaching departure from Broomhill. "You know that I would forfeit my life and all I possess to save you pain. Spoken or unspoken, it matters little: you know that the world holds but you for me; that you are and ever have been the absorbing passion of my existence."

Donald knelt beside her on the moss-covered turf, the love in his deep-set eyes pleading for the rash words he had uttered, while a stray sunbeam, glinting through the foliage, illumined his up-turned features. This loyal and true lover of hers might move a stonier heart than that which was beating so tumultuously within her, she thought, as her gaze rested fondly and sadly on him for a few moments.

"You will not lessen my trouble by talking to me in this manner," she replied, in a hard, metallic tone.

"You rebuke me, and perhaps you are right. I do not try to exonerate myself; but what is the use of keeping up this farce between us? Even if your grief had not wrung the truth from me, you must have known for weeks, for years past, that you are dearer to me than life itself."

Donald was pale with passion to the lips as he spoke. He was reckless of all cost; his voice was hoarse and broken with the love which was only conscious of itself, and the response which it craved. He was prepared to risk all, lose all, forsake all, so long as he could look upward into Evelyn's eyes and read in them a passion equal to his own.

"I must leave you, for I dare not listen to you," said Evelyn, trembling with emotion, and her eyes swimming with tears, while she extended her hand to him to bid him good-bye.

"You must and shall listen to me," said Donald, heedless of her words, and intoxicated by the touch of her hand and the dreamy languor that veiled the brilliance of her eyes. "Evelyn, you love me. I know it, and, by heavens, you are not going to let that mockery of a

marriage stand between us any longer.
What if I am legally bound to a cunning
mad woman ? I only gave her the shelter
of my name out of pity, and I swear by
my love for you that she was never my
wife except in name. The walls of the
asylum do not part me from her more
effectually and fully than my own inclination. Evelyn dearest, I have never
spoken of the past. I have never reproached you for breaking faith with me.
I never asked to pry into your secrets or
to find out the hand that connived at our
separation. I loved you, though you
deserted me. Your very treachery was
powerless to steel my heart against you.
False, cold, and mercenary though I
deemed you, the universe held but you,
and you alone, for me, and I would not
have ceased to love you if I could. Oh,
Evelyn ! what necromancy did you use to

bind me to you in such complete and abject thraldom?"

These supplicating words seemed wrung from Donald by some resistless force, and, flinging himself forward in the intensity of his emotion, he threw his arms round his cousin. She neither repelled him nor caressed him. The fierce conflict that was swaying within deprived her of all sense, and she sat voiceless and motionless.

"Evelyn," continued Donald, raising her cold hands to his lips and kissing them passionately, "I place my life again in your hands, to do what you like with it. It is at your mercy, as it was long years ago at Monkhurst, and I offer you the same unchanging love that I did then."

"Do not speak to me of love," interrupted Evelyn, with a harsh, hysterical

laugh. "It is a meaningless word for
me. I have never felt it. If you trusted
me, I should betray you; I should repay
your devotion by falsehood. You have
found me heartless and mercenary in the
past; I should be the same in the
future."

"By heavens, you are maligning yourself!" said Donald, springing to his feet
as though he were stung by an adder.
"If you swore you did not love me, I
should not believe you. Love such as
ours reveals itself in a more subtle lan-
guage than words. You are fighting
with yourself; I know it by your looks.
You are doing violence to all that is
tender, and true, and womanly within you.
For the sake of some old-world notions
of right and wrong, will you be content
to wear away your life in perpetual
sadness? for, mark my words, you will

be as powerless to escape the memories of the past as I am."

Evelyn made an effort to rise, but Donald held her still, and she felt too enervated for any resistance.

" In the freshness of my early manhood, I chose you for my wife, and loved you with all the strength, all the fervour, all the intensity of my nature. There was some good in me in those days, Evelyn, and all that was purest and noblest within me was consecrated to you. I had neither the wealth nor the expectations of Randolph de Ruthvyn to offer; but, had you blessed me with your hand, I should have carved out a future not unworthy of you, and I think we would have been happy together. If inclined to scorn me now, remember that my love is not the passing fancy of the hour. It is not the passion of a voluptuary. Remember that, if you had been true to me, we should have been one flesh and blood in the sight of God and man for the last fifteen years. Let it end one way or another now, for it is beyond my powers of endurance. My life has hitherto been one long suffering, but there is a limit to it. Evelyn, though your past actions condemn you even more than the words that have just fallen from your lips, I trust you still. I supplicate for your love as in the days of old; but, by the heavens above, if you reject me, I shall leave you, and never cross your path for good or for evil again. '

" I do reject you," cried Evelyn, freeing herself from his grasp, her head thrown proudly back, her eyes dilated, her voice rising and quivering in the air. " I wish you would leave me. I wish you would go, and never cross my path again."

Donald fixed his eyes upon her as she spoke, and saw that her face was white, calm, and impenetrable as the face of the dead, and knew that she had pronounced a decision from which there was no appeal.

"You shall not find me an importunate suitor," said he, scornfully, letting his eyes linger on the pale, fair features of his cousin for a moment or two longer. "I am quite willing to rid you of my presence, since it is so disagreeable to you. I need scarcely say again that our parting now is final." His voice was hoarse as he answered, with a harsh, discordant sound vibrating through it, and it struck upon her like the chill of cold steel.

In another moment he was gone; the

network of foliage screened him from her sight, and she realized the bitter truth that they had not only parted, but parted in anger. Would eloquence or persuasion have prevailed to bring about an amicable parting between them? she wondered, as she recalled her unkind words, and reproached herself for having denied her love for him. She had overstepped the boundary-line of actual necessity, and had been wantonly cruel to him, she thought.

Evelyn made an effort to walk home, but staggered as she advanced a few paces, and sank in a half-fainting condition among the ferns. A deadly stupor was creeping over her; the trees looked like phantoms. There was a rushing sound in her ears, and, looking round, she realized the impossibility of walking to the castle. She knew that there was

a gamekeeper's lodge within quarter of a
mile, and that, if she could reach it without fainting on the way, she could rest
there while a messenger went for the
pony-carriage. She dipped her hand-
kerchief in the cool water of the stream,
bathed her eyes and throbbing temples,
and then summoned up her remaining
energies for the walk. As the stream
was shallow, she crossed it by some
stepping-stones, instead of going round
by the little bridge; but before she
reached the other side, the giddy sensation returned, and, missing her footing,
she fell in an unconscious state among
the ferns and rocks, cutting her wrist in
the effort to save herself. Evelyn had
never fainted before, and the gradual
return to life was quite a new experience
for her. It was a strange sensation, the
reawakening of her deadened senses, and

she mistook the dim, unreal sights and sounds for a dream.

She was asleep, she thought, and in her dreams Donald had come back to her. His arms were round her, and she was assuring him that her cruel words were false, for that she had never ceased to love him. She could feel his breath upon her cheek, the warm clasp of his hand within hers, as she clung closer and closer to him. Was it a dream, the sweetest dream that ever cheated her senses, or was it a reality? Was Donald in truth beside her, wooing her back to life by the warmth of his caresses; or was the dark, passionate face that was bending over her a mere phantom of the brain?

His voice broke the spell, and called back her wandering senses. Opening her eyes wide, she recognized her cousin, and

a swift, vivid colour dyed her cheeks, as
she hid her face upon his breast, ashamed
of the love she had at first denied, and
then had so fondly and vehemently
admitted.

"You do not send me from you now,
Evelyn, my beloved; you will let me
stay with you always?" said Donald,
pressing his lips against her cheek.
"When you drove me from you," continued he, in answer to her questions,
"I wandered about half frantic through
the wood, and found myself again at the
river-side, though I thought I had gone
in an opposite direction. I saw you
cross the stones and fall, and came to
your rescue, prepared for another scold-
ing; but my darling was tired of being
unkind to me."

"Yes; I am tired and weary—very
weary," she murmured, in a scarcely

audible voice, and closing her eyes as though she were again lapsing into the faintness of insensibility. Donald was alarmed as the colour died so quickly from her face, while her hands were trembling in his own.

" You must rouse yourself, Evelyn dearest, or you will be seriously ill. If you cannot walk, you must let me carry you to some place where we can get assistance. The skirt of your dress is wet from the river, and your feet must be damp."

" Let me rest a little longer, just a little longer ; I feel so very tired still," pleaded Evelyn, faintly.

" Shall I leave you for a few moments, while I go in search of assistance? Surely there must be some lodge or cottage near, where I can get a messenger to send to the castle ? " asked Donald, eagerly.

"No, no; you must not go away. If you leave me, you will not find me again," said Evelyn, her cousin's last words effectually rousing her. "I will lean on you until we get to the gamekeeper's lodge, which is not far off; but I must be your guide, as, by your own account, you have already lost your way." Evelyn spoke with apparent gaiety, but her smile was forced, and there was an expression of sadness upon her face.

They walked together through the tangled coverts, fragrant with wild flowers and the lingering scent of hawthorn, and then entered the leafy aisles of the forest, where the light was subdued, and all was dim and solemn as in a sanctuary. In that hushed and quiet solitude there was no sound but the voice of Donald, pleading eloquently for the passion which had been more the bane than the delight of his existence.

Evelyn checked the hot, impetuous words, and laid her hand lightly upon his arm. She knew that at the end of the next long avenue of elms they should part, and who could tell whether they would ever meet again?

"Donald," she said, pausing in her walk, while her eyes grew humid as she gazed upon him, "this spot reminds me of the woods near Monkhurst, where we parted years ago. Let us renew our vows here; let these aisles be our temple, and let us swear to be faithful to each other until death divides us."

"Yes, dearest," said Donald, bending over her and kissing her unrebuked. "This canopy of foliage, with the blue arch of heaven beyond, shall be our temple. It is the noblest and most sacred of all edifices; but what shall I say more than I have already said to convince you that, if you unite your life to mine, I will prize it as the divinest gift upon earth?"

"Nothing, Donald. I know you love me, and, be it for good or evil, you know now that your love is returned. It was treachery parted us in the past, and I have never loved any one but you. It is a whim, a mere caprice of mine, that I wish you to tell me again that you will be faithful to me, and I want you to give me your ring as a token of your promise. I can get it made smaller for myself afterwards."

"You are welcome to it, my darling," said Donald, taking off his signet-ring and placing it on the fourth finger of her left hand; "but it is not half good enough for you. I should like you to wear a ring of my own selection, a diamond or a sapphire hoop."

"I won't have any but this. You have worn it yourself, and it will be dearer to me than any other; and, Donald, I want you to promise that, whatever happens in the future, you will not think harshly or unkindly of me. You will remember that I have confessed my love, and promised to be true to you until the last hour of my life. You condemned me in the past, but you know the thoughts of my heart now, and you will be very merciful to me." The lids drooped softly over her eyes, and a sadness stole over her face as she spoke, but Donald mistook the meaning of the words and the cause of the sadness. "This narrow pathway leads to the lodge, and you must not ask to come further with me," said Evelyn, pausing again in her walk, and

pointing to a passage scarcely distinguish-
able among the shrubberies. You will go
home direct to the castle, and tell them
to send me the phaeton, will you not?"
she continued, looking at Donald with a
smile. "You cannot mistake your way
now, as we are out of the intricacies of
the wood."

"I may come back in the phaeton for
you, surely?" said Donald, dreading that
he was getting his *congé* for the rest of
the day.

"I would rather you did not ask to see
me any more to-day," said Evelyn, looking down, and twisting nervously a
pocket-handkerchief which she held in
her hand. "I scarcely like to tell you
how weary I feel, lest I should distress
you. I think I shall fall asleep when I get
home, and perhaps I shall dream of you
and our strange marriage service to-day."

"Evelyn," cried Donald, his voice trembling with excitement, "you know that I would give all I possess to be as we were years ago, to be privileged to seek you for my own lawful wife ; but you will try to be happy under the present circumstances, darling, trying as they are ? There are lands, bright, sunny lands, preferable in many ways to England, where you will be safe from a breath of slander, and where we shall think the world well lost for the happiness of being together. The years will not be long either, dearest, until a legal union shall unite us, for disease such as poor Helen suffers from undermines the strength, and the doctors say she will not be long-lived."

"To wish her dead is to be a murderer," said Evelyn, sighing, and averting her eyes ; "and you would not wish to be such, dearest," she continued, in a low voice. "We must not try to shape or alter our lot in life according to our own wishes; we must accept it as it comes, and do the right, whatever happens. You will be my own true and loyal lover to the end, *sans peur et sans reproche.*"

As Evelyn spoke, she looked at her cousin again, and allowed him to press a long, lingering kiss upon her lips. It stirred no passion within her. It was a kiss such as the living might give to the dead, for all that was human within her was frozen at that moment. Then, silent and tearless, she tore herself from him, and hastened towards the lodge; while he, not doubting that he would see her the following morning, wended his way to the castle to do her bidding.

CHAPTER VI.

IT was barely eleven by the castle clock
the following morning when Donald stood
at the entrance of the great square hall,
with its vaulted roof and panelled walls,
and inquired of the powdered lackey
who lounged in the doorway if Mrs. de
Ruthvyn was in. The hours had passed
slowly since he had parted with Evelyn.
He had spent a restless night, and had
greeted the dawn with the same delight
that a captive hails his freedom. It was
the dawn of a day that would restore him
to his beloved, he fondly believed, never
more to be separated from her. There

was no need to study etiquette any longer, no need to put off the visit until the afternoon, or even midday. The barriers of reserve were broken down at length, for she had confessed her love for him. One thought, one hope, one wish animated them both, and she was doubtless looking forward to the hour of meeting with the same rapture that he was. His very breath was taken taken away when the powdered youth told him, with a languid drawl, that Mrs. de Ruthvyn had started for London by the nine o'clock train from Stockford, and had left Delamere a little after seven. Donald stared at him in blank astonishment, as if he had said something utterly incredible. He was about to rush past him to Evelyn's morning room, with the wild hope that he would find her there, in spite of the man's statement, when he was met by

the old butler, who gave him a note,
which, he said, Mrs. de Ruthvyn had left
for him that morning. A chill came over
Donald, and a terrible foreboding of disappointment, as he took hold of it. He
went out into the gravel sweep in front
to escape the inquisitive looks of the
servants, and, tearing open the envelope,
read the following :—

"I have run away, dearest, as I had
not courage to say good-bye. It was
cowardly of me, but I could not spoil
your happiness yesterday. I endured the
bitterness of parting in silence, for even
when you were planning our future, I
knew that what you wished could never
be. The day will come when you will
know that I have done right, though it
may be hard for you to admit it now.
For myself, I dare not say what I feel ; I
only know that I am yours entirely and

for ever, and that, though we may not see each other again, the words we spoke yesterday shall be as binding upon me as any marriage service."

Donald read no more. With a fierce and bitter oath, he tore the letter in shreds and threw it to the wind. "She thinks to dupe me still," he thought, as he laughed a harsh, discordant laugh. "She does well to talk of honour, when her whole life is a piece of acting. I might have known that her soft mood yesterday was but a repetition of the farce at Monkhurst, when she looked up in my face and kissed me, while she was plotting treachery against me in her heart. She need not fear that I will trouble myself to follow her. From this hour I shall forget her very existence."

As Donald hurried along, with his brow as black as thunder, and scarcely knowing where he was going, he ran against Fleurette, who had just come from the garden. She had a bunch of creamy roses in her hand, and looked charmingly pretty in her pale pink cambric frock, with her golden hair floating in the wind.

"What is the matter?" she said, startled at his wild looks, and laying her hand caressingly on his arm.

"Nothing," he replied moodily, trying to shake her off. "I am going away," he added, in a more conciliatory tone, "and cannot stay to talk with you now, Fleurette."

"Take these with you; they will remind you of Delamere," continued Fleurette, pressing the flowers upon him.

"I believe you will be sorry for me, little one," said he, noticing the tears that had gathered in her eyes. "You will miss me for a while, but you will be a grown-up woman before we meet again— that is, if ever we do meet—and you will have become as selfish and hardened as the rest of your sex."

Donald refused the flowers. They were Evelyn's favourite roses, and were too closely associated with her to be anything but hateful to him in his present humour. Pushing them from him with an impatient gesture, he kissed Fleurette, and then strode away in the direction of Broomhill.

CHAPTER VII.

IN order to follow the fortunes of Teresa, who is not the least important character in this narrative, we must go back to the cold and blustering month of March. It may be remembered that Bernard's directions, on parting with her at her lodgings, were, that if she did not hear from him the second morning after his departure for Daleshire, she was to proceed to Paris, and carry out his instructions with regard to Fleurette. Bernard did not act with his usual discretion during his visit to Delamere. The brougham having failed to meet him at the station, he arrived at the castle in a very bad temper, and in

an insolent tone of voice bade Evelyn
account for her niece's absence. The
former refused to give him any information about the child, and haughtily re-
quested him to leave Delamere. Before
taking his departure, he contrived to have
an interview with Kate Penthony, from
whom he learnt that Fleurette, for whose
sake he had quarrelled with Evelyn, was
at school in the neighbourhood of Stockford, and that she came home every week
from Saturday till Monday.

This news, surprising as it was, only
served to irritate him afresh; for, on looking at his watch, he perceived by the late-
ness of the hour that Teresa had already
started on her journey, and that no telegram would reach her until she arrived in
Paris. Bernard returned to London by
an evening train, and lost no time next
day in telegraphing to Teresa.

The telegram, which was addressed to
Mademoiselle Maroni, Hotel de Lille et
d'Albion, was as follows :—" Return as
soon as this reaches you. Will write
particulars to Oxford Street." It arrived
at its destination at one o'clock, the same
day that it was despatched; but Mademoiselle Maroni was out when it came,
and when it did reach her she was not at
all inclined to obey its summons. The
fact is, she was thoroughly happy in her
new quarters, and, though not forgetful
of the respect due to the future wife of
Mr. Bernard Waldstein, was enjoying a
flirtation with a tall, swarthy-looking
Frenchman, who had been conspicuous
in his attentions to her since the previous
evening. He was lounging about the
coffee-room when she arrived, and was
evidently fascinated at first sight. As the
evening wore on, he ventured to address

her, having an idea from her general appearance that his attentions would not be distasteful. Teresa was a little guarded at first, and Monsieur Dufour—for such was the Frenchman's name—confined his attentions to procuring books and papers for her amusement. He became more venturesome the following morning. By a little diplomatic arrangement with the waiter, he contrived to breakfast at the same table with her, and they were soon engaged in lively conversation with one another. Monsieur Dufour expatiated on the beauties of the French capital, and, as it was *terra incognita* to Teresa, he offered to escort her to some of the leading places of resort. The Italian girl, though a good deal flattered at the new and unmistakable conquest she had made, felt some misgivings at accepting the offer of her companion without letting

him know that her hand and affections
were already engaged. She thought it
would be prudent to draw the line at
tête-à-tête drives in the Bois de Boulogne.
She blushed, looked charmingly confused,
and faltered some words to the effect
that her intended husband had entrusted
her with a commission which would
occupy the morning, but that she would
be very happy to avail herself of Monsieur Dufour's kind offer for the afternoon.
The Frenchman sighed, looked unutter-
able things, and cast vindictive glances at
the opposite wall, as if the unknown
fiancé of his charmer stood somewhere in
that direction, and could be annihilated
with a scowl. Then, gulping down his
café noir absently, he asked Teresa, in a
tragic tone of voice, when the event was
to come off. The latter was a little perplexed by the question, and had to admit

that no definite time was fixed yet; but it was a marriage worth waiting for, she added significantly. Her *fiancé* was not only a gentleman in the truest sense of the word, but a nobleman ; she would be a baroness by-and-by, and own extensive property both in Germany and England. If Teresa had wished to snub her new friend, she could not have succeeded more effectually.

Not half an hour before he had been boasting to her that he was proprietor of the handsomest hotel in Rouen. He was decorating and furnishing it in the newest style, he told her, and had come to Paris for the purpose of consulting the best artists. He had talked in a high-flown strain for the purpose of ingratiating himself with the Italian girl, who, according to her own account, was only forewoman at a millinery establishment in Oxford

Street ; but this news of her engagement
made him feel very insignificant. It
deprived him of all his self-importance,
and quite took away his breath. Teresa
regretted that she had been so communi-
cative on the subject of her marriage,
when she returned to the hotel three
hours later, and found that Monsieur
Dufour was not waiting for her according
to promise. She could scarcely blame
him, however, as she was nearly two
hours late, Bernard's commission having
occupied more time than she expected.

She had a long and tiresome search for
the Convent of St. Cecile. There had been
a delay in getting admittance when she
arrived ; and, after a weary interval spent
in a small room looking out on a gloomy
courtyard, a solemn-faced nun made her
appearance with Mrs. de Ruthvyn's card,
which she returned to Teresa, saying that

she must be under some mistake, as
neither the abbess nor the teachers knew
any one of the name. Teresa was to
some extent relieved at not finding the
child; she had disapproved of Bernard's
scheme from the first, and had lately felt
that the charge of Fleurette would be a
great restraint upon her own movements.
Still, she was annoyed that her day had
been wasted on so profitless an errand,
and she was disappointed, on returning
to the hotel, to find that she had missed
her appointment with Monsieur Dufour.
The latter made his appearance in time
for the *table d'hôte*, and restored Teresa's
equanimity by producing two tickets for
the Bouffes Parisiens, which he presented
to her, with a request that she would
make use of him as an escort.

It was during dinner, and just as the
Frenchman was giving Teresa some slight

sketch of "La Belle Hélène," the piece which was to be performed at the theatre, that a waiter brought in a telegram and laid it beside her. The porter had omitted to give it to her on her return from the convent, although it had been waiting for her some hours. Teresa frowned angrily, and pushed the telegram towards her companion, vowing to herself that even if Bernard were ready to marry her next day, she would not forego the pleasure of her visit to the theatre. She was so disappointed at this sudden ending of her sojourn in Paris that she did not notice the excited looks of her companion, as he scanned the telegram and read the name, "Bernard Waldstein."

"If this is from your *fiancé*, I know him!" said he, eagerly. "He was staying with me at my hotel in Fondi. He came there to make private inquiries about an English gentleman whom I knew intimately many years ago."

"You must be mistaken," replied Teresa, with a laugh and a shake of her head. "You are not likely to have met Mr. Waldstein, or to have been intimate with any of his friends."

"But I have met him," rejoined her companion, "and I can describe him accurately to you, if you wish." Whereupon Monsieur Dufour drew a not very flattering description of his rival, and Teresa was forced to admit that in some points he was correct. "I am certain, also," continued the Frenchman, emphatically, "that Mr. Waldstein's inquiries were prompted by self-interest. His motives were not all pure love for Mr. de Ruthvyn. I. would venture to bet half a dozen pair of gloves with you, that the errand he sent you on to-day was in some way connected with Mr. de Ruthvyn and his daughter, who is to be very rich some of these days."

"I don't see that it concerns you, at all events," replied Teresa, with a haughty toss of her head. "If Mr. Waldstein chooses to entrust me with a confidential commission, it is because I have known his family for many years. Mrs. de Ruthvyn is his sister, and I have lived in her service at Delamere Park for over seven years." Teresa, in her surprise at finding her new friend so familiar with the name De Ruthvyn, forgot that she had stated to him not many hours before that she was forewoman at a millinery establishment.

The Frenchman, however, took no notice of her inconsistencies, but continued to examine the telegram. "A light dawns on me," said he, suddenly starting to his feet and rubbing his hands gleefully, while his companion gazed at him with surprise. "Not only am I acquainted with Mr. Bernard Waldstein, but, if I am not mistaken, I have met relatives of yours years ago in Italy. I did not remember your name when you first mentioned it, but now that I see it coupled with that of Mr. Bernard Waldstein, it reminds me that many years ago, when I lived with Mr. de Ruthvyn, or Monsieur Delille, as he chose to call himself then, both he and I passed some hours in a cottage not far from Mola di Gaeta, with people named Maroni, who were in the fishing trade. We had a wounded officer with us, and as soon as we could move him we took him to Terracina in a closed carriage. Mr. de Ruthvyn never forgot the kindness of those people."

The Frenchman looked steadily at

Teresa as he spoke, and noticed her deepening colour and confused looks. She recollected vividly that past episode, but was determined to ignore it.

" My people have been settled in Marseilles for over twenty years," she replied, venturing this untruth in the hope that she had altered as much as Monsieur Dufour in the intervening years.

She had no desire that he should associate her with the poverty-stricken abode where her childhood had been spent, and Monsieur Dufour understood what was passing in her mind at a glance, and adroitly changed the subject. He remembered the bare-legged, scantily dressed peasant girl, with the dusky skin and brilliant black eyes, who had attended the wounded man at the cottage, and had little doubt that she and the elegantly

attired damsel who was sitting beside
him now were one and the same person.
He did not think the worse of Teresa for
her lowly origin, but it made him doubt
the intentions of Mr. Bernard Waldstein.
Having told an untruth, Teresa was resolved to adhere to it, and was more silent
than usual, lest she should get into fresh
difficulties. Monsieur Dufour's allusion
to an heiress rankled in her mind, and
aroused vague misgivings within her.
Could Fleurette be the heiress, and could
her prospective wealth be the reason for
Bernard's deep and unaccountable interest? she wondered. Was she the child of
Monsieur Delille, whose real name Teresa
now knew to be De Ruthvyn? There
was some mystery connected with the
child, and she was determined to unravel
it; but she would dismiss the subject
from her mind to-night, and enjoy herself

thoroughly. She felt more at her ease with her new friend since she heard of his connection with the De Ruthvyn family; and although she would not give him the satisfaction of admitting that they had met before, she treated him as affably as if they were old friends. The lively gaiety of the Bouffes eclipsed the recollections of the Alhambra, although Bernard had been with her at the latter place. She could talk of nothing but the gorgeous appearance of Schneider while partaking of the *recherché* supper afterwards at the Palais Royal, for which Monsieur Dufour had the pleasure of paying.

After some persuasion on the part of her friend, Teresa consented to remain another day in Paris. She had as yet seen nothing of the city, as her first day had been entirely taken up by the visit to the convent, and she admitted that it would be vexatious to return, knowing as little of the wonderful city and its sights as when she came. The Frenchman escorted her to the Louvre, Palais Royal, and Bois de Boulogne. They drove to the latter place in an open carriage, and dined at the Café Madrid. Teresa was enraptured with all she saw, but wisely resolved to return to England that evening.

Monsieur Dufour was very pleasant as a companion for a day's excursion. But she had no idea of throwing over so eligible a *parti* as Bernard for him; besides, she was anxious to get back to see what had become of Fleurette, and to discover Bernard's real motives for wishing to have the care of her. She resolved to be true to him until she had positive proof of his treachery, and not all the cajoling of the

Frenchman availed to worm from her
the secret of her visit to Paris. She
admitted that it was business connected
with the De Ruthvyn family, but would
say no more on the subject.

Monsieur Dufour had the melancholy
satisfaction of seeing Teresa off on the
first stage of her journey. He drove
with her to the Gare St. Lazare, looked
after her luggage, and procured a comfortable carriage for her, but had to content himself with the promise, that if ever
she wanted a friend she would have recourse to him. She would find him at
all times ready and waiting, and he
would be only too proud to defend her
if she ever found herself in a position of
danger or difficulty. Teresa was inclined to laugh at her friend's vehemence ;
but she put his address safely by in her
purse, and as the train moved out of the

station, and they waved a parting adieu to each other, she had a misgiving that he would be called upon to redeem his promise.

CHAPTER VIII.

NEARLY four years have passed since Fleurette and Donald Stamer were such good friends at Delamere, and she is approaching her seventeenth birthday. She has been at a boarding-school in Brussels for the last year and a half; and, though she cannot be classed among the most diligent of the pupils, she has made enough progress in the fine arts to please Evelyn, who is very anxious that her son's future wife should not be deficient in any accomplishment, and who has very fastidious views on the subject. Bernard, on the plea of relationship, has contrived to pay an occasional visit to the school, when he has done his best to make himself agreeable. He has had no opportunities of seeing her when home for the holidays, as Evelyn is not inclined to forget his rudeness, and he has not been invited lately either to Delamere or Monkhurst; but he consoles himself with the thought that, if he succeeds in his designs upon Fleurette, whom he looks upon as the future mistress of Delamere, it will matter very little to him whether his sister becomes reconciled to him or not.

Fleurette did not like the change to Brussels at first. She felt sad and lonely for many months, and did not seem inclined to make friends with either the schoolgirls or teachers. Her only consolation was writing home, and counting the days to the next vacation, when she would return to her beloved Delamere; but before a year had elapsed, the accidental meeting with an old lady on board the Antwerp steamer led to circumstances which completely reconciled her to her new life.

It was on her way back to Belgium, after the Christmas holidays, that Fleurette first attracted the attention of Miss Bouverie. The latter, though an old maid, was matronly in her appearance. She had a sweet smile, a tall and dignified figure, and her placid, handsome features bore no traces of disappointment or crosses of any kind. The world had gone smoothly and well with her, apparently, and in what manner she had escaped matrimony was a mystery to her friends. Miss Bouverie on first perceiving Fleurette thought she was travelling alone, as she was roaming about

the deck in an independent fashion;
while Clarice, who was accompanying
her as far as Antwerp, where she was to
be met by one of the governesses, sat
demurely on one of the benches, busy
with her knitting. Fleurette took a
fancy at first sight to the grey-haired
lady who addressed her so kindly, and
they were soon talking as familiarly as
if they had known each other for years.
They were mutually surprised on discovering that they lived at a short distance from one another. Miss Bouverie
resided at a place called Driancourt,
three miles beyond Brussels, and she
promised to call at the school, and
get leave for Fleurette to spend the
first half-holiday with her. Fleurette
was enchanted with the idea, and admitted that, much as she liked Brussels,
the half-holidays were very dull and

monotonous. She preferred the school
in Didscombe much, for many reasons.
There were such lovely walks in the
neighbourhood; and then, she was so
close to Delamere that she could always
return there from Saturday until Monday.

Miss Bouverie looked astonished when
Fleurette mentioned Delamere. "Tell
me your name again, my love," said she,
putting on her spectacles and looking
at Fleurette intently. "Ah yes; De
Ruthvyn. It ought to have made an
impression upon me. I have reason to
remember the name."

"Do you know my Aunt Evelyn?"
asked Fleurette, who was rather discon-
certed at the old lady's manner.

"I have never seen her, but have often
heard of her as Evelyn Leith. Friends
of mine knew her intimately before her
marriage. She was a beautiful girl then,

but haughty and ambitious to excess.
She is content now, no doubt, that her
son has inherited the Delamere property."

Fleurette did not like the way Miss
Bouverie spoke of her aunt; and though
she changed the subject, and did not
refer to her again, she had an idea that
they must have offended each other in
some way in those bygone years.

On her arrival at the school, Fleurette
was all impatience to write home, and tell
of the invitation she had received; and,
though some of the schoolgirls predicted
that nothing more would be heard of the
old lady, she was as good as her word.

Not a week later she arrived at the
school, in a handsome carriage drawn by
a magnificent pair of bays. She introduced herself to Madame de Lange, upon
whom she made an agreeable impression,

and had no difficulty in obtaining Fleurette leave of absence for the rest of the
day.

Driancourt was a fantastic - looking
château, situated on a slight declivity in
the midst of prim Dutch gardens, which
were gaudy with tulips and hyacinths,
and other brilliant-looking flowers, the
day Fleurette paid it her first visit.
There was an old-fashioned English
garden at the rear, where roses and
carnations bloomed in wild luxuriance,
and where the trees and shrubs escaped
the pruning-knives of the gardener, and
were, consequently, of a less grotesque
shape than those of the front lawn.
Miss Bouverie was fond of birds and
domestic animals of all kinds. She had
a large aviary, a dozen dogs of different
species, besides numerous cats, who all
lived together in the greatest harmony.

Fleurette was introduced to them in turn, and took a special fancy to a large retriever, who lay basking in the sunshine on the hall door steps.

Miss Bouverie seemed pleased at the notice she took of the retriever. He belonged to her nephew, she said, and was consequently a great favourite of her own. He was a most sagacious dog, and had become so attached to her during the four years she had the care of him, that she would find it hard to give him up when her nephew came home. The latter was with his regiment in Malta, but was leaving very soon, and would be at Driancourt some time in the early summer. She hoped Fleurette would meet him before she went back to England for the vacation.

Fleurette was not long in perceiving that this nephew Charlie held a very

prominent place in Miss Bouverie's affections—that she loved him, in fact, as
devotedly as her Aunt Evelyn loved
Raymond; but she formed a wrong impression about his age at first, as she
took it into her head that he was about
the age of her cousin. It was not until
a subsequent visit that Miss Bouverie
undeceived her by showing her his photograph, a large framed picture which
hung in the old lady's bedroom, and
which, according to the latter, was taken
twenty years ago. It represented a very
handsome young man in the uniform of an
hussar regiment. He was twenty-one at
the time, Miss Bouverie said, and had
just entered the army.

Fleurette was disappointed to find that
this nephew, of whom she had heard so
much, and whose arrival she was some-
what interested in, should be quite an

old man. Forty-one was a very advanced age, according to her ideas. He must be very nearly as old as his aunt, she thought. She liked the face in the picture. It seemed familiar to her, though she could not think of whom it reminded her, and she found herself wondering what change had come over it in the twenty years.

It was not surprising that Fleurette appreciated the change from the dull boarding-school to a bright, luxurious home like Driancourt, but it was strange that a staid, elderly lady should take pleasure in the companionship of so young a girl. Miss Bouverie, however, differed from the generality of old ladies, and liked the society of young people, as a rule, much better than men and women of her own age. It soon became a settled thing that Fleurette should

spend Sundays and half-holidays at
Driancourt, and before a month had
passed, she felt herself as much at home
in the Belgian château as if she had been
brought up there.

One Saturday, towards the end of
April, Miss Bouverie's carriage having
called as usual at the Place Bellard for
Fleurette, the latter arrived at Driancourt,
to find her hostess and all the domestics
in a state of unusual bustle and confusion.
The maid-servants were hard at work,
polishing mirrors which were already
spotless, and putting up fresh lace cur-
tains in the sitting-rooms ; while the
gardener and outdoor men were brushing
the lawn and flower-beds, and cutting
down every offending daisy that appeared.
Miss Bouverie herself was conveying a
pot of lilies of the valley from the con-
servatory to the drawing-room.

"You are just come in time to help us. We are all as busy as bees. I had a letter from Charlie this morning, and he will be with us about nine o'clock this evening. The dear fellow is coming home direct to me, though he had an invitation to stay with some Italian friends at Turin."

"Do let me help you with the flowers, and take a rest on the sofa, or you will be quite worn out before your darling Charlie arrives," said Fleurette, throwing off her hat and cape, and taking the lilies from her friend, which she placed on an ornamental stand. "Mathieu will show me the other flowers you wish moved, and you shall see how beautifully I will arrange them."

"No, dear; you have got on your pretty cambric frock, and I won't allow you to soil it with the flower-pots. You may help me to arrange the cut flowers, if you like; but ask Madelon first to lend you one of my big aprons. These flowers have all to be put in the vases and jardinières, and it will keep you busy for an hour," continued Miss Bouverie, pointing to a large basket full of exotics.

Fleurette skipped off, and soon returned with a large holland apron on.

"You are pretty safe now," said the old lady, scrutinizing her costume through her spectacles, to see if any portion of her frock was visible. "Now, you must not tire yourself too much, for I want you to be in good voice, and to sing your new song for Charlie; I hope you brought it with you. He is very fond of music, and has had but little of it lately, I should think."

"Oh dear, Miss Bouverie! don't ask me to sing to him to-night; I should feel so nervous. You remember how I broke down the last evening you accompanied me in my song, and I have not practised it once since. Signor Bonoldi does not encourage me much, either. He says I ought to keep to exercises and scales for another year."

"Don't mind him, my dear. You sing 'Ritorno ch'io t'amo' like an artist; and I think I am as good a judge as he."

Miss Bouverie dined at the unfashionable hour of five, as she thought early hours more conducive to health; and Fleurette had scarcely finished the arranging of the flowers, when the dinner-bell rang. About an hour afterwards she returned to the drawing-room, and was about opening the piano to play over the accompaniment of her song, when she noticed a photograph-case lying on the instrument. She opened it without much hesitation, and found that it contained two likenesses. One was Miss Bouverie's nephew, and was the facsimile of the photograph hanging in her bedroom. The other likeness in the case was coloured, and represented a young lady of about three or four and twenty. The face was oval; the eyes of a steely hue, set close to the nose, which was high and well formed. The hair was red, though the brows and lashes were dark and beautifully pencilled. The skin was of alabaster whiteness; but the feature which spoilt the whole face was the mouth. It was a cold, cruel mouth, with thin, compressed lips, and Fleurette took a dislike to the portrait at once. She was looking at it, and wondering who it could be, when Miss Bouverie walked in.

"Do tell me whose is the likeness side by side with your bonnie Charlie. I don't admire it at all, and yet it ought to be pretty; but there is such a cunning, malicious expression about the mouth."

" She is a relative, a niece of mine, and was very handsome some years ago," said Miss Bouverie, gravely, taking the photograph from Fleurette.

" I had no idea she was your niece. What must you think of me for abusing her ?" said Fleurette, in a crestfallen tone.

" She is only a niece by marriage, and was never a favourite of mine, so don't look distressed, dear. I know you did not mean to offend me. As you have seen her likeness, I will let you a little into the family secrets. You may often have wondered why I chose to live here instead of in my own country. It was not from love of the locality, although I have become fonder of Driancourt than

I expected. When I came to settle here twelve years ago, it was to consult a celebrated doctor about this lady," said Miss Bouverie, pointing to the photograph. "She was in bad health at the time, but has become much worse since, and she lives in the same house with the doctor now, to be more completely under his care."

"I might have known she was delicate," said Fleurette, sadly. "Her features are so sharp and attenuated. Is she consumptive?"

"No; worse than that. Her mind is quite astray; but you must not ask me any more questions about her," replied Miss Bouverie. "I have told you more than I intended, and if you want to please me, you will never refer to the subject again." As Miss Bouverie spoke, she locked up the offending picture in a drawer, and then opened the piano. "Get your song now, Fleurette, and let us have a little practice while the daylight lasts. You will find my spectacles in the work-basket."

The old lady had scarcely played the opening chords of the accompaniment, when the sound of approaching wheels attracted Fleurette's attention, and she ran at once to the window.

"Well, you are incorrigible," said the former, with a good-natured smile. "I don't wonder Signor Bonoldi is provoked sometimes. What have you run away for?"

"There is a carriage coming up the avenue, with luggage on the top. I am certain it is your nephew Charlie, coming earlier than you expected."

"I scarcely think so," said Miss Bouverie, rising and moving towards Fleurette. " It is more likely to be a vehicle from the nursery at Boitsfort ; I have been expecting some plants to arrive all day."

"I don't think these are plants," rejoined Fleurette. " You can see the carriage through the openings of the trees distinctly, and there is a cart following with more luggage."

" You are right, child ; you are right," replied the old lady, in eager tones, as the vehicle came more fully in sight. "It is Charlie, and no mistake." Then, without another word, she hurried out of the room in a state of breathless excitement.

" I wonder what he is like ? " soliloquized Fleurette, as soon as she found herself alone. " I hope he won't monpolize all Miss Bouverie's time, and dislike my coming here. I dare say he is a crotchetty, ill-tempered man, like Sir

Robert Ellmore. India generally gives people liver disease, or something to make them cross and disagreeable. I shall have to sing for him, too, though I don't half know this song. I wish I had not brought it, and then Miss Bouverie could not have asked me to sing it."

Thus musing, Fleurette sat down at the piano, and began to sing in a soft undertone; but her song was destined to be again interrupted, for she had scarcely played a few bars, when, hearing footsteps behind her, she looked round, and was startled to perceive Donald Stamer. He advanced to meet her with a careless smile, while Fleurette's astonishment was so great that it deprived her for a few moments of speech.

" I am so glad—so very glad to see you!" she exclaimed, in breathless tones. " Where have you come from? Are you

going to stay? Have you come with
Miss Bouverie's nephew?" She asked
these questions with the eager impetuosity
of childhood, while she made no attempt
to conceal the delight that beamed from
her expressive features.

" I should scarcely know you, Fleurette," said the new-comer, detaining her
slender hand in his for an unnecessary
length of time. "You have grown so
tall, and you are quite a young lady now,
with your long petticoats and your hair
up. I only heard a few weeks ago that
you were here, and was half inclined to
write to you, but knew I should be in
Brussels almost as soon as the letter."

" I had no idea Miss Bouverie knew
you," said Fleurette, in a bewildered
tone. " I suppose you have come with
her nephew, and that you are a friend of
his?"

"You are trying to perplex me with your questions, Fleurette. What do you mean by asking me am I come with her nephew? Miss Bouverie has no nephew but myself."

"You are not in earnest," replied Fleurette, looking at her companion with wide-open eyes, as though she were trying to read the truth of his assertion upon his countenance. "Her nephew's name is Charlie, and he is a great deal older than you are. He is quite an old man."

Donald burst out into a loud fit of laughter. "So you take me for an impostor, a second edition of Tichborne? It is a delicious joke! Come here, you unbelieving little mortal, and be convinced." As Donald spoke, he drew her beside him on the sofa. "Look at this letter," continued he, taking an envelope from his pocket, which Fleurette perceived at a glance was addressed to Colonel Stamer in Miss Bouverie's hand-writing. " See how the old lady begins her letter. She has a weakness for calling me Charlie, as it was my grandfather's name, though I am Donald to the rest of the world. Are you satisfied now about my identity, or do you want more evidence? " said he, in a bantering tone, while Fleurette gazed perplexed at the letter.

" It is so strange that Miss Bouverie never asked me had I met you, and yet she knew I lived at Delamere," said Fleurette, in a musing tone. " I can almost fancy we are back there," added she, wishing to change the subject. " It seems only a few days ago when we used to walk together to Mrs. Grisney's farm-yard, to see her chickens and ducks. You are not the least changed, though you say I am so altered."

"Four years make more difference at your age than at mine, but you are improved; you have grown prettier than ever, so you need not mind, my child. Yet for all that, I would rather have you as you were. You were such a lovable little girl, and now you are stately and stand-off. I suppose you would consider it quite *infra dig.* to give me a kiss, though you gave me one at parting, and promised me one when next we met?"

Fleurette blushed at the very thought, and, moving further away from her companion, protested that she had no recollection of the occurrence.

"Four years are long enough to obliterate that little episode from your mind, and I must not tease you; but tell me, Fleurette, what made you think Miss Bouverie's nephew was such an antiquated fossil?"

"It is not fair to tease me on that subject either, so I shall leave you now, and not give you the chance of chaffing me any more." Fleurette laughed as she spoke, and though Donald did his best to detain her, she ran towards the door and made her escape, just as Miss Bouverie entered.

CHAPTER IX.

FLEURETTE was not less of a favourite with Miss Bouverie after Donald's arrival. She continued to spend Sundays and half-holidays at Driancourt, and the severest work at school was brightened by the prospect of happy hours spent at the château. As Easter drew near, Miss Bouverie suggested that she should spend it with her, instead of at Delamere. The vacation was so short, that it would not be worth while crossing the sea, and running the risk of getting sick; and Fleurette agreed with her. Somehow, the young girl's affection for Delamere was insensibly diminishing, and she was in unusually high spirits when Evelyn wrote to say she might accept Miss Bouverie's invitation.

The day before the school broke up, and while waiting for the carriage to call for her, she was taking a stroll with a favourite schoolgirl. They had scarcely reached the playground, when a servant followed Fleurette, and told her that a lady was waiting to see her in the visitors' room. Fleurette returned to the house, rather aggrieved at being interrupted, and was met at the entrance by a stout, well-dressed female, who threw her arms round her neck, and almost smothered her with kisses.

" My darling ! my sweet mademoiselle ! How well you look, and what a big girl you have grown ! Have you no word of welcome for your poor Teresa, or have ou quite forgotten her ? "

Fleurette knew the voice, and, as soon as she could free herself from the arms that encircled her, she recognized her former maid. The latter had developed a considerable amount of *embonpoint* during the years that had elapsed since she and Fleurette had met, and had become much fuller in the face.

" It was cruel of her dear mademoiselle to let two years pass without coming to see her. Nothing but the dread of meeting Mrs. de Ruthvyn had kept her from going to Delamere to get a glimpse of her nursling. She could not yet forget the unkindness she had met, after all her years of service; but surely Fleurette, who knew her address, could have come to see her occasionally.

Though Teresa spoke in this complaining manner, it was evident she had not taken offence, and a kiss from Fleurette brought back her smiles.

" You can't look angry, Teresa, though
you are trying your best; and how becoming that pretty olive-green cashmere
gown is, with all the beautiful embroidery !
Madame Melfort must pay you a good
salary, to enable you to dress as you do."

"Ah, I have good taste, mademoiselle,
and that is everything. Madame Melfort
knows it too, and sends me to Paris
twice a year to choose her fashions. I
get my own things there at the same
time. This dress, however, was a present.
It would have been quite beyond my
means. It was bought for me at the
Compagnie Lyonnaise by a gentleman,
who will be a very near relative in a
short time." Teresa blushed as she
spoke, and began to take off her gloves
in a hurried and nervous manner.

"A gentleman who will be a near
relative soon ! Ah, that means you are

going to be married!" said Fleurette,
with a laugh. "You may as well tell me
all about it," she added eagerly, taking
hold of Teresa's hand. "I suppose this
pretty turquoise which you wear on the
fourth finger is the engagement-ring.
Make a full confession to me at once."

"I did not intend to tell you so soon,"
replied Teresa, with a beaming countenance; "and yet there is no reason I
should keep it secret. I am going to be
married to Monsieur Paul Dufour, a rich
hotel-keeper at Rouen. I shall be mistress
of a large and handsome establishment,
and shall have more money than I know
what to do with; but Paul is so good and
fond of me, that I should be contented if
he were poor."

"This is good news indeed," said
Fleurette, shaking Teresa by the hand,
and kissing her on both cheeks in the

continental fashion. "You must give
me due notice when the wedding is to
take place, that I may send you a handsome present. Would you like something
in the way of jewellery, or a useful present
for your house?"

Teresa did not answer for a moment or
two. She kissed her dear mademoiselle
again, and said she would write to her
after she had consulted Paul.

Fleurette was among the favoured
boarders at Madame de Lange's, and had
a bedroom to herself. She took Teresa
up there after a little while, and had tea
and cake served to her. There was a
good deal more talk about Paul, and
Teresa gave a graphic account of her first
acquaintance with him, omitting to tell
Fleurette that she herself was in any way
connected with her visit to the Hotel de
Lille et d'Albion. Paul had fallen in love

at first sight on that occasion, and had remained faithful and devoted to her ever afterwards. It was impossible, in fact, to throw him off, and, though not much in love with him at first, his perseverance had won the day.

"But, mademoiselle," continued the Italian girl, with strange eagerness, as soon as she had sufficiently expatiated upon Paul's merits, "you must not think of having a lover for many years to come. I am thirty, and you are only seventeen. You must not dream of marrying for a very long time."

Fleurette laughed heartily. "Rest easy in your mind, Teresa; I have never given the subject a thought. I am not grown up yet, and don't intend to be for a long time."

"That's right, my child," continued Terosa, placing her arm round the young

girl's waist in a caressing manner. " You
have a pretty face and charming manners,
and I am glad of it ; but adventurers will
be on the look-out for you for the sake
of other attractions, of which you know
nothing at present, and I want you to be
warned of them in time."

" What attractions do you mean,
Teresa? I wish you would be less
mysterious. If you mean money, I don't
believe I have any ; at least, nothing to
signify. Do explain yourself."

" You shall know everything by-and-
by, my dear mademoiselle ; all I want is
to warn you. Paul and I know more
about you than you think ; but he would
be angry with me if I were even to give
you a hint yet awhile."

" Paul ! " repeated the young girl, in a
bewildered tone. " Do you mean your
Paul? What can he know of me ? "

"He knew you when you were a baby, mademoiselle. He lived with Monsieur Philip de Ruthvyn, the kind gentleman who adopted you, and was with him until he died."

"Is this really true?" said Fleurette, her expressive countenance suddenly illumined with joy. "Where is this Paul of yours to be found? He must tell me all he knows about my baby days; I am literally dying to see him. I feel quite the heroine of a romance, too, with all this—this mystery you have been hinting at."

"We shall come to see you in less than three months' time, depend upon it. Till then remember my warning, and bear in mind that it is specially directed against a gentleman you know very well—I mean Mr. Bernard Waldstein, Mrs. de Ruthvyn's brother. Spurn him with the same contempt that you would the lowest menial at Delamere, if he should dare to ask you to marry him." Teresa hissed out these words in a venomous tone of voice, and her face was livid with rage.

"Dear Teresa, you are so excited, and say such strange things, that I am inclined to think your head has been turned by the good fortune of captivating Monsieur Paul. Why should Bernard want to marry me? It is too absurd! I look upon him as an uncle."

"He is no uncle of yours, mademoiselle. He may be uncle to your cousin Raymond, and you may call him so too, but it does not prove any relationship. He is free to ask you to be his wife, and, mark my words, he will do his best to make you marry him. I have warned you now, and feel easier in my mind; but you will get me into great trouble if

you repeat any of my words. Don't
mention my name, or a syllable that I
have told you, when you are writing
home to Delamere, and say nothing about
it to the lady you are going to stay with.
Paul would be angry with me, and I
know you would not wish to get me into
trouble."

"I shall be as silent as the grave, if that
will suit you," replied Fleurette, laughing; "but when am I to have my proposal? I shall dream of it by night and
day until it comes. You must tell me
what it is like, as you have had one so
lately. Will Bernard go down on his
knees, kiss my hand, and swear eternal
adoration?"

"I see you are chaffing now, mademoiselle. You are taking it as a joke, so I
may as well go away, and say no more
about it."

" No, no ; you must not go. I never was less inclined to chaff. I am dying of curiosity to know what you mean. You really must stay." As Fleurette spoke, she pushed Teresa back in the chair, from which she had risen.

" I cannot remain any longer, dear child. I am staying with Paul's sister, and I promised her I should be back in less than an hour. She and her husband live in the Rue Neuve. They keep a restaurant there, and are expecting some friends this evening, so I could not disappoint them."

" I will let you go, then, as you are staying in Brussels, for we shall often see each other. Driancourt is not more than an hour's drive from the town, and you must come and spend a day with me."

" Alas ! mademoiselle, I have already

outstayed my time, and must return to-morrow; but we shall meet soon again. I shall be my own mistress in less than three months, and free to find you wherever you are."

"You must stay, at all events, until the carriage comes. We shall pass through the Rue Neuve, so I can leave you at home."

As Fleurette spoke, she heard the rumbling of wheels, and, looking out of the window, perceived Miss Bouverie's brougham entering the courtyard.

"I have been delaying you, mademoiselle," said Teresa, with distressed looks, "and now perhaps your things are not packed. You have to change your dress, too."

"My luggage is all ready, and I am not going to change my dress until I arrive at Driancourt, so don't worry yourself. You have not detained me in the least, dear Teresa."

As Fleurette spoke, she opened her wardrobe, and put on a dark blue felt hat, and feather corresponding in colour with her dress. Teresa eyed the latter garment critically, and put a pin here and there in the drapery of the overskirt to suit her own fancy.

" I see, you want my eye over you, my dear child. If I had the superintending of your dress, it should have been made in quite a different fashion. I could have altered the style while we were talking here together, if I knew you were going to wear it."

" You must come and dress me some of these days for my wedding, as you have such a good idea of style. Remember, you have fixed the date yourself—at twelve years from this, so you must not

be disappointed if I shall have fallen off
in my looks."

As Fleurette spoke, she took a rapid
survey of her figure in the tall cheval
glass, and, notwithstanding Teresa's disparaging remarks about her dress, was
pleased with the *tout ensemble* which she
saw reflected. She then ran down the
stairs, followed by Teresa, and, having
said good-bye to Madame de Lange, took
her seat beside the Italian girl in the
brougham, and ordered the coachman to
stop at the Rue Neuve, No. 40.

CHAPTER X.

FLEURETTE did not trouble herself much about Teresa's warning. It sounded too ridiculous to be of any importance, and she dismissed it from her mind almost as soon as she said good-bye to the Italian girl at the Rue Neuve. Marriage was as yet a far-off event in her life, she imagined, and could never be associated with Bernard Waldstein. She was not blind to the fact that her aunt looked forward to a time when a closer tie would unite her to her cousin Raymond. They had played at being engaged lovers since they were children, and during her last visit to

Delamere Raymond had shown her very
plainly that the play had become earnest
so far as he was concerned. They had
loved each other all their lives. He was
more devoted to her than ever brother
was to sister, and it would not be very
difficult to drift into a nearer and dearer
relationship with him as years went by.
There would be no rapture, no emotion,
in such a marriage. It would be the
same love that she had known for years,
only called by another name; but they
might be far happier than many married
people. Fleurette had heard stories of
quarrels and separations, but she felt
certain that nothing of the kind would
disturb the serenity of their future lives.
Fleurette had no reluctance to this calm
and passionate courtship until a few
weeks ago, when an indefinable change
came over her. Since then, she tried

to persuade herself that Raymond only loved her as brother. He was scarcely nineteen yet—a mere boy, who would change his mind a few years hence. He would travel by-and-by, see the world, fall desperately in love with some one else, and his mother would be equally delighted. Fleurette felt strangely wise and old for her seventeen years, and had completely changed her ideas about age.

She was unusually agitated as the brougham drove up the avenue to the château, and expected every moment to hear the bark of Colonel Stamer's retriever. He would bound up to the carriage, she thought; and then his master would follow, take her hand in his, and welcome her back to Driancourt. But a bitter disappointment awaited her. The retriever was more silent than usual, she noticed. It was not until the

brougham was quite close to the hall
door that he came to greet her in a very
lazy fashion, and he was not followed by
his master. Miss Bouverie met her on
the steps, kissed her with her usual affection, and, leading her into the house,
complained of being very lonely, as her
nephew was away; he had gone to
Louvain, and would not be back for three
or four days. Fleurette reproached herself for the chill feeling of disappointment
which swept over her at these words of
Miss Bouverie. Why should Donald's
absence or presence make such a cruel
difference to her? Why should Driancourt look so blank and desolate, when her
hostess was there still, smiling and kind
as ever, unchanged from those former
days when Fleurette asked no better
company.

Two uneventful days passed, bringing

no tidings of Donald, and Fleurette was
beginning to think he had gone to Paris
or London, and that she would not see
him once during her holidays. In the
mean time, she was doing her best to
enliven her hostess. She sang her
favourite songs, helped her with her
crewel work, and was unusually vivacious
and talkative. The afternoon of the third
day, the old lady was dozing on a sofa in
the drawing-room, the dogs were all
taking their afternoon siesta, and Fleurette, after vainly attempting to read one
of the Tauchnitz novels, put on her hat,
and strolled into the old-fashioned garden
behind the house. It was a day when
mere existence was a pleasure. The birds
were singing a lively chorus among the
laurels, the warm air was perfumed with
a thousand scents, and the tender green
of early spring decked the budding foliage.

"How lovely the flowers are, and what an enviable existence is theirs!" thought Fleurette, with a sigh, as she bent over a bed of daffodils, looking fairer than any of the spring flowers herself in her dainty dress of cream-coloured foulard.

This neglected garden was a favourite retreat of hers. Untrained roses spread in wild luxuriance; starry magnolias peeped among the verdure; flowering shrubs lent a variety to the foliage; and, at a distance, a grove of chestnuts offered a shelter from the sun. There were seats beneath their spreading branches, and not a fortnight ago Fleurette had sat there with Donald Stamer, while he was giving her an account of his adventures during the march to Coomassie.

Fleurette looked sadly at the empty seats, and thought how enchanting it would be if Donald suddenly returned,

and spent the rest of that bright and
beautiful afternoon with her. Why had
he gone to Louvain? she wondered. Was
he related to the mad lady who lived
there under the care of a doctor, and was
his visit connected with her? Fleurette
had brought a basket and scissors to the
garden with her, the gardener having
given her leave to cut what she liked,
provided she did not encroach upon his
favourite flower-beds in the front lawn.
She had collected a choice variety, and
was about to return to the house, when,
hearing footsteps, she looked round, and
perceived a figure through the trees
which at first sight she mistook for
Donald Stamer. Her heart beat wildly,
her colour came and went; but the next
moment the gentleman came fully in
sight, and she recognized Bernard Waldstein.

" You here! " she exclaimed, with a look of profound astonishment, as she dropped the basket and scissors, and advanced to meet the new-comer, her face clouding with disappointment.

" Have you no better welcome than that for me, Fleurette ? " said Bernard, fixing a glance of undisguised admiration on her, while he attempted to draw her to him—an attempt, however, which she successfully repelled.

" Do you know, I have had great difficulty in finding you here. This garden is such an abominable labyrinth," he continued, feeling suddenly aggrieved at her coldness. " I was just going to give it up as hopeless, when I caught sight of your dress through the trees."

" I have scarcely yet recovered my surprise at seeing you here," said Fleurette, looking wonderingly at her companion, while the colour slowly returned to her cheeks as her agitation subsided.

"Why are you so pale, Fleurette? I don't like that transparent look in your complexion; you don't seem nearly so strong and well as when I saw you four months ago. I hope they have not been overworking you at that miserable school. I protest against the brain work imposed upon young girls nowadays," continued he. "It is a most pernicious system, and proceeds altogether from vanity on the part of the principals; but, thank goodness, they won't have you to experimentalize on much longer."

"I like Madame de Lange extremely," said Fleurette, bridling up at Bernard's disparaging remarks upon her teacher. "She does not overwork me at all, and I should be very sorry to leave Brussels. Does Aunt Evelyn say that I am to

return home ? " Fleurette had become
pale again with anxiety, as she asked this
question.

" You forget that Evelyn and I are not
on speaking terms ; but if you are tired of
the school, as no doubt you are, I can
easily arrange for you to leave. I will
make it all right with your aunt afterwards, and you need not fear getting into
trouble."

" Surely you would not encourage me
in such a naughty act as to run away
without leave ? " said Fleurette, with a
merry laugh, while she bestowed an arch
glance on her companion.

Bernard was puzzled at her mood, and
doubtful whether he ought to chance his
fate at once, or wait until he had oppor-
·tunities for a little more love-making.
How charming she was, and what a
perfect beauty she had turned into ! he

thought, as he gazed at her fair face, and congratulated himself upon his chance of winning such a bride. Even if she were not the heiress he knew her to be, her personal attractions were enough to turn his head. Fortune had favoured him in every respect, and his very quarrel with Evelyn, which at one time he thought so disastrous, was working for his good, as it enabled him to carry on his courtship without her knowledge.

"I assure you, Fleurette," continued he, in an excited tone of voice, "if a thousand pounds had been placed in my hands, I could not have been better pleased than when the servant told me at the school that you had come here for your vacation."

"What difference can it make to you whether I am here or at home?" asked Fleurette, mischievously lifting her violet eyes, and meeting the bold stare of her companion in a questioning manner.

"Sly little girl, to pretend you don't know," said Bernard, making a second attempt to place his arm round her waist, while his features assumed a leer which was the reverse of becoming. "Don't pretend to be too innocent, Fleurette. If you are not a baby or a simpleton altogether, you must have noticed the unusual interest I take in you, and you must know that my reason for wishing you to be here is the chance that it gives me of being with you. Thanks to my sister's ill temper, I am debarred from seeing you at Delamere, and I naturally feel an interloper in Madame de Lange's establishment for young ladies. What about the old woman here? Is she at all hospitably inclined? Is there any chance of her asking me to stay? Stamer and I are very good friends, and it is just possible on that account that she may ask me to remain until he returns. What fun you and I would have, if the old lady took it into her head to be amiable! I hope she will ask me to dine, at any rate, as I have walked here from Brussels, and feel as hungry as a hawk."

Fleurette launched at once into a panegyric of Miss Bouverie's amiable qualities, glad of an excuse to divert the conversation from herself. Teresa's warning had something in it, after all, and Bernard's looks, no less than his words, made her feel nervous. The proposal was imminent, she felt sure, and he would be down on his knees among the flowers if she did not make an escape in time. What should she do if Miss Bouverie come unexpectedly upon them, and discovered his arm round her waist, or his hand clasping hers? And do what she would, she could not shake him off.

Miss Bouverie was most kind and hospitable, and would be certain to ask him to remain, Fleurette assured him. It was enough to be a friend of her nephew's to gain favour in her sight. As she spoke, she was rapidly nearing the château, accompanied by Bernard, and before they reached the gate leading round to the lawn they were met by the hostess herself. She had awoke from her doze, very much refreshed, and, hearing that a strange gentleman was with Mademoiselle Fleurette in the garden, thought it prudent to reconnoitre the ground and find out who he was.

Bernard bowed courteously when Fleurette introduced him, and said he was an intimate friend of Colonel Stamer's. He had come to see him, and was sorry to hear that he was not at home. He thanked Miss Bouverie in the most affable manner, both in his own and his sister's name, for her great kindness to their ward.

Fleurette was too polite to contradict him, but she opened her eyes very wide at this sudden assumption of guardianship ; still, she was amused at the cleverness and diplomacy of his speech, and the result was what both she and he expected. It was enough for him to be a friend of Miss Bouverie's dearly-beloved nephew, to be made welcome at Driancourt. The invitation was at once given to him to dine, and his hostess added that, should he care to exchange the liveliness of the town for the seclusion of her château, she hoped he would bring his portmanteau from the Hotel de Russie the following day, and take up his abode with them for the remainder of his sojourn in the neighbourhood.

While Miss Bouverie and Bernard were exchanging civilities, they continued walking towards the entrance of the château. Fleurette kept behind them for a few moments, and then slipped away unobserved. She did not join them until a few minutes before dinner was served, and, in the mean time, Bernard had been through the stable and all round the grounds with Miss Bouverie, and had confirmed the good impression he had made upon her at first sight. He was evidently fond of the open air, his hostess thought, for, as soon as dinner was over, he proposed another stroll upon the lawn. The old lady suggested that the season was not far enough advanced for late rambles.

" But this is an unusual evening," he

persisted. "Look!" said he, throwing open the window, and turning round to Fleurette, "did you ever see a more enchanting night?"

Fleurette threw a light shawl over her shoulders, and stepped out for a few moments. The lawn was flooded with moonlight, and not a breeze was stirring. The flower-beds looked like fairy circles upon the sward, and the dim recesses among the trees seemed so strange and unreal in their fantastic and sharply defined outlines that she was almost tempted to explore them. Turning round to speak to Bernard, however, her eyes met his, and she at once decided to remain indoors.

"It is cold to-night, and the lawn looks damp and ghost-like," she said, shivering as she spoke. "Come inside, and we can have a game of chess instead. It will be far more amusing. Miss Bouverie will lend us her carved chessmen, and we will see whether you or I will get checkmated first."

Bernard returned most unwillingly to the drawing-room, where he found Miss Bouverie busy with her knitting at the fire, and a dark shade passed over his features, as he felt how completely he was checkmated for the present. There was little hope of a *tête-à-tête*, since Fleurette set herself so deliberately against it. She was doing it on purpose to annoy him, he felt sure. The nonchalant way she was arranging the chessmen provoked him so much that he could scarcely conceal his irritation; but he was relieved when Miss Bouverie rose from her chair, and, saying that she had forgotten some of her wool upstairs, left the room, closing the door after her.

"Why are you so stiff and unkind to me, Fleurette?" said he, suddenly looking up at his companion. "Was it not enough to avoid me the whole afternoon, without refusing to take a turn on the lawn with me when I asked you? I don't believe that you were cold. Come into the next room, at all events, where we can say a few words without being overheard by the old lady. She will be back again in a few moments, I suppose, and we can play our game just as well in there." As Bernard spoke, he swept the chess-men with an angry gesture into the box, and walked into a small boudoir off the drawing-room.

"You are in a capricious mood to-night, Bernard; but I am prepared to humour you. We will play in any room you like, only don't scold. I hate being scolded." Fleurette guessed what was coming, but Bernard looked so comical in his anger that she felt more amused than nervous.

" Sit down beside me here, Fleurette, and let us have a quiet time to ourselves," said he. " I am not going to scold you or reproach you any more. Of course you are too young yet to share my feelings in all their intensity, and I must not expect it ; but tell me, dearest, that I am not disagreeable to you—that you will try to like me, and that some day you will make me supremely happy by becoming my wife."

Fleurette smiled, and, leaving the sofa, leant against the back of an arm-chair, facing her companion. " Raymond says I am to be his wife in a few years ; Aunt Evelyn wishes it too, and I cannot marry you both."

" They have forestalled me, then. I

might have guessed as much," said Bernard, springing off the sofa and approaching her. " Early as I am in the field, I have a rival already."

" But perhaps I may not marry him, after all. I may prefer being led by my own feelings," said Fleurette, with one of her sauciest smiles.

" Then I need not fear him. You do not love him? Oh, say so again, dearest! I might have known that such a mere boy as he—a bookworm, too, entirely devoted to his studies—could not inspire you with a romantic passion."

" You are quite mistaken. I love him dearly, though it may not be with what you call a romantic passion. I love him much better than I love you, at any rate," said his tormentor, with a mocking laugh.

" Do not trifle with me, Fleurette, on

a matter that is life and death to me. You are no longer a child; you ought to try and discuss seriously so important a subject, and not laugh as if you were half idiotic."

" It is the only way to treat anything so silly and absurd; but I will be as demure as you like, if you change the subject. You are my guardian, so I am sure you take an interest in my studies. Let me show you my essays. I got the prize for French prose last week."

" Don't mind the essays now; they may be ever so beautiful, but I can't waste my time with them. Remember, I must leave this in half an hour, as I have a long walk back to Brussels, and I want to have something settled before I leave. Fleurette, have you any idea of what it is to love?"

A fugitive glow suffused the young girl's cheeks as the question was put to her. Yes, she knew what love was, she thought. She had felt that strange mingling of pleasure and pain which is called "love," but she did not feel at all inclined to discuss the subject with Bernard Waldstein. His words, however, had given rise to a train of thought, and she remained lost in reverie for a few moments, leaning on the back of the chair, and almost unaware that Bernard had her hand in his, and that he was gazing at her with looks of admiration. It was of Donald she was thinking, and her thoughts were so occupied with him that she was not surprised when a door opened in front of her, and he suddenly stood before her. He made a movement at once as if to retire.

"Miss Bouverie told me I should find

you both in the drawing-room ; but I am afraid I have disturbed a very interesting *tête-à-tête*," said he, advancing, after a moment's hesitation, and shaking hands with Bernard and Fleurette.

CHAPTER XI.

DONALD STAMER was not pleased with the turn that affairs had taken in his absence. He had no liking for Bernard Waldstein, and was irritated beyond measure at finding him domiciled at Driancourt ; but he would probably have got over his objection to him, if circumstances had not led him to suppose that he and Fleurette were lovers. Not that he was in love with the young girl himself. Even if honour had permitted him to think of her, love, in the ordinary sense of the term, was a thing impossible for him—at least, so he believed. He only looked upon her as an interesting and engaging child, whose artless talk amused and enlivened him. His heart was so seared with the repeated disappointments of life that her very freshness and inexperience made her irresistibly charming to him. She roused him from his fits of moodiness, and he felt a greater interest in her than he had ever hoped to take in womankind again ; but the interest was fatherly in its nature, and the affection at its very warmest was widely different from the love which he had given Evelyn. It seemed, however, as if fate grudged him this small amount of interest and amusement. Fleurette would no longer care to waste her time in his company; another would monopolize her, and, instead of the pleasant hours which he had spent with her, he would have the disagreeable sensation, whenever he came across her path, of being in the way.

He was in the library one afternoon, looking over the newspaper, which had just arrived from London. Miss Bouverie had gone to a little cottage by the riverside, to visit some of her poor people. Bernard and Fleurette were on the lawn outside, and Donald was half inclined to join them, not finding much in the papers to interest him, when his eye was suddenly caught by a paragraph announcing the approaching marriage of Evelyn, widow of the late Randolph de Ruthvyn, with the Earl of Ilberry. There was nothing very startling in the announcement. It was short, and very quietly put in, yet the blood surged through Donald's brain, and the hand that held the paper shook with emotion. It recalled to his mind an announcement of a similar kind which he had read many years ago, the only difference being that in the present instance the marriage was yet to come, and in the former it had already taken place.

"The Countess of Ilberry will sound very well, no doubt," he soliloquized. "What matter that the bridegroom is over sixty years of age, and has not one personal or mental quality to recommend him—a coronet will amply compensate for other deficiences; money was the attraction on the former occasion."

Donald tore out the offending paragraph, crushed it in his hand, and pushed it into his pocket, unwilling that any one should see it and comment upon it to him. Though so ruffled by the news, his thoughts had not been much occupied with Evelyn since he parted with her at Delamere four years ago.

Infuriated with her then, for the decision
she had come to, he had almost hated
her for a while. Even when the heat of
his emotions had subsided, and he had
calmly looked back upon the episode in
the wood and the disappointment which
followed, he gave her no credit for re-
jecting him. He saw nothing high-
souled or moral in her conduct. She
was cold and heartless, and would let
him suffer the tortures of the rack rather
than damage her position in society, he
believed.

Until he met Fleurette, he had heard
nothing of any of the Delamere party,
except what reached him through Fred
Brandreth, who was all through the
Ashantee campaign with him, and who
naturally repeated any home news to his
brother-officer. There was a day, shortly
after their arrival on the African coast,

when Donald had been in a particularly bitter mood against Evelyn, and had expressed his feelings pretty freely to his companion. Young Brandreth silenced him by taking a very unromantic view of the case. It was all nonsense, he said, to make Evelyn a kind of scapegoat for everything that had gone wrong in his life. His marriage with Miss Carlyle was the circumstance that had doomed him to a solitary, unloved existence, and not the fact of having been engaged to his cousin for a few months many years ago. If death dissolved the tie that bound him to his present wife, he would probably find how frail were the bands that united him to Evelyn. "The love that devastated his life," Fred insisted, was all moonshine. In the natural course of things, it must have burnt itself out years ago. A hundred

chances to one, if he were free to-morrow,
instead of marrying Evelyn, he would
choose some one else.

Donald had muttered something uncom-
plimentary under his breath to his friend
at the time, and had taken care to avoid
the subject afterwards ; but the words returned to his mind to-day, and he found
himself pondering over their meaning.
If free to marry, would his interest and
admiration for Fleurette develop into a
warmer feeling? he asked himself. He
knew that he could prove a very formid-
able rival to Bernard, if he chose. He
would quite enjoy the fun of entering
into the lists with him, of watching his
discomfiture as he lost ground day by
day, and of winning all Fleurette's smiles
and loving glances for himself. It would
not be very difficult to make her love
him, he imagined ; but what was the use

of thinking about it ?   He was not free;
and, even if he were so, he was not at
all sure of his own feelings.

Donald opened the window that led
to the lawn, feeling a stifled sensation
from the heat of the room.   He stepped
out on the terrace, and, walking a little
distance, perceived Fleurette seated under
a cedar tree.   As the obnoxious Bernard
was not with her, he made up his mind
to monopolize her for a while himself, and
find out whether she had heard anything
of Evelyn's marriage.   The fact that she
was spending her holidays at Driancourt
suddenly struck him as conclusive proof
that Evelyn had something unusual in
prospect.

Fleurette was so intently engrossed
with her book that she was not aware
of Donald's approach until he was quite
close.   Throwing away his cigar, he took

the vacant seat beside her; but his thoughts were so abstracted that he scarcely noticed the glad look of surprise that sprang into her eyes. It was the first time that he had taken any special notice of her since his return, and she felt in a transport of joy. He had looked so coldly at her lately, and had been so formal in his manner, that she was persuaded she must have offended him; but he was going to be his old self again, and she would be supremely happy. Donald, however, was not his old self; he was low-spirited, and not inclined to talk. He took the book from her, and, turning over the leaves, looked at Raymond's name, which was written in a schoolboy hand on the fly-leaf.

"Do you remember what good friends you and Raymond were long ago? You had it all settled among yourselves that you would be engaged lovers by-and-by, and now, it seems, you have changed your mind."

Fleurette blushed deeply, and, not knowing Donald's thoughts about Bernard, was quite in the dark as to what he was alluding.

"Raymond and I are just as good friends as ever. I had a long letter from him two days ago from Oxford. Just fancy! he is reading eight hours a day. But he is to join Aunt Evelyn next week at Monkhurst, and they are going for a trip to the Trosachs."

"I thought your aunt was at Delamere," said Donald, in as nonchalant a tone as he could assume.

"She says she will never live at Delamere again until both Raymond and I are of age. She will have to wait two years for him to be twenty-one, and four for me. I can't think why she should want me to be of age."

" Don't you think it very likely that Evelyn will marry again, before either of you are of age ? She will live at her husband's place then, and not at Delamere."

"Aunt Evelyn is much too fond of Raymond to think of marrying again ; and she is perfectly infatuated about Monkhurst. There are memories connected with it which has made it very dear to her, she says. Her father and mother lived there, you know."

Donald was about to produce the paragraph, and ask Fleurette what she thought about it, when he saw Bernard approaching. " Here comes your indefatigable friend, Fleurette. I thought I should have had you to myself for half an hour, but I must resign you now."

"Why should you go away?" said Fleurette, looking round at him with a pleading expression, and placing her hand upon his arm to detain him. "Stay; do stay. I should fifty times rather you were with me than he."

"Little flatterer! you would spoil me if I listened to you," said Donald, rising from the seat and standing where the sunlight fell full upon his stalwart form and clearly-cut features.

"Bernard has been down to the river to see about a boat," rejoined Fleurette. "Would it not be pleasant if we all three went together? I could steer, while you both rowed."

"We should get sunstroke to a dead certainty on such a broiling afternoon. Seriously speaking, it is too hot for such an exertion as rowing, Fleurette. If you asked me to go with you alone, now, you might tempt me ; but to be cramped up in a small boat with Bernard is another thing."

Donald took out his cigar-case as he spoke, and Fleurette knew that he was going. He wanted to get away, it was evident, and she would not humble herself any more by pressing him to remain with her ; but he did not go yet.

" Will you do something to please me ? " he said, in an insinuating tone, while he took her hand in his. " Don't go out boating with Bernard, unless Miss Bouverie can go with you ; and I don't believe she can this afternoon, as she is visiting her pensioners at the village. Play billiards or croquet with him instead. It will be much pleasanter, as there is no shade on the river, and you have a long hot walk before you can reach it. Now you are angry with me for giving my

advice unasked," he continued, noticing
the tremor of her lips and the dark shade
that passed across her features.

Fleurette was too mortified to speak.
" He does not care for me, or he would
not send me off so coolly to play billiards
or croquet with another," she thought ;
and, dreading that she would betray more
than she intended, she snatched her hand
from him, and walked away without
vouchsafing an answer to his question.
" What right has he to dictate to me ?
I shall go in the boat, just to show him
that I don't care for him," she soliloquized, as she advanced to meet Bernard,
who, to judge from his beaming countenance, had succeeded in his errand.
While about ten yards' distance from
him, she suddenly changed her mind, and
turned down a narrow walk, thickly
bordered by trees, intending to return

through a succession of similar paths to the château, and thus avoid Bernard until she felt in a better temper for his society. She had not advanced many paces, when, hearing footsteps, she turned round, and perceived that he had followed her.

" Can you not leave me alone ? Why do you persist in following me ? " she said, in a petulant tone of voice, forgetting that not an hour ago she had been quite in the humour for the expedition. " I have changed my mind about going in the boat. The sun is much too hot, and it would make me sick."

" Who could have put such an absurd idea into your head ? You have been in such a delightful humour all day, Fleurette, and you will not become cross now to spoil it all," said Bernard, with a beseeching look.

"If I do go, it will be to suit my own purpose, and not to please you," she answered, defiantly; "and, before I go, you must promise not to open your lips on the subject of love. You have thoroughly wearied me with it to-day already."

"How saucy she has become all of a moment!" said her companion, raising his eyebrows and gazing in mock surprise at her. "You are a complete weathercock, Fleurette ; you are not in the same mood two minutes together. But, come along, and I will agree to anything you like. We will discuss nothing but scientific subjects, if you wish."

The weather was unusually warm for May, and Donald was right in saying that the walk would be hot and unpleasant. After leaving the demesne, they had a stretch of dusty road, and the path then led through fields, unprotected by any shelter. The sun was sinking gradually towards the western sky before they reached the lonely village at the river-side, where the boat was moored. Bernard soon detached it from the little nook that formed a rude landing-place, and before many minutes had elapsed he and Fleurette were floating in it along the rippling surface.

"Do you know, Fleurette, I am going to invest in a yacht. I am in treaty for a perfect little gem, and it will be mine, I hope, before the summer is half over. My first cruise shall be to the Ionian Islands. Can you imagine a more delightful spot for a honeymoon?"

"I did not think you went in for Byronic romance," replied Fleurette, sarcastically.

"You have misjudged me, then; I am

of a most poetic temperament. What can be more romantic than this scene, which I will now picture to you? I am stretched under the awning of my yacht, with the cloudless skies of the Levant above me; perfumed breezes are wafted from one fair island to another; and a vision of beauty, with lustrous eyes, peachy complexion, and golden brown hair is by my side, looking upon me with kinder glances than she ever bestowed upon me before."

"You are breaking the promise you gave me when I entered the boat," interrupted Fleurette, hastily.

"By no means; I am only describing my future wife. Why should you take the description to yourself? You have refused me, and it would be illogical to presume that you were to be the lady of the yacht."

Fleurette smiled, and, to relieve herself from the awkwardness of the remark, asked Bernard to sing a boat-song.

"I must look over my *repertoire*, and have one when next we come out. As I cannot sing, I will tell you a piece of news instead. Unfortunately, I cannot tell it to you without touching a little on the forbidden topic, but I will be as brief as I can. You tell me that you are engaged to your cousin Raymond, and that this engagement has dated from your childhood." As Bernard spoke he looked at Fleurette, who turned away her head, as if unwilling to listen. He had ceased rowing, and let his oars skim lightly upon the surface. "Now, your own words show that you are not in love with your cousin, and it would be preposterous to think of forcing such an engagement upon you. To be sure, he has wealth,

large estates, and they may be an attraction ; but suppose I were to tell you that
in a few years' time Raymond's wealth
would melt away from him—suppose it
were proved that the estates were not
his, never were his, and that I, in the
mean time, could put you in possession of
a large fortune, would you be inclined to
look more kindly upon me ? "

"I will not waste a thought upon
anything so absurd," said Fleurette,
angrily. "What could happen to Raymond's money ? Why should his estates
melt away ? You are only trying to
frighten me, and it is very unkind of you.
It is true that we have been engaged in
some absurd way since we were children ;
it was a whim of Aunt Evelyn's, I think.
But Raymond may change his mind before
·he comes of age, and he is quite welcome
to do so ; he will be equally generous to

me, I am sure. But whether he releases me or not, I could never marry you. It pains me to say so—indeed, it does; but I am delighted to hear of your good fortune, and hope you may meet some one who will love you even better than you love me."

" Vastly obliged; you quite overpower me with your good wishes," said Bernard, a dark shade passing over his features.

As he spoke, he made a few strokes and veered the boat round to the point from which they had started. Within the last hour the sky had become over-cast; dense masses of clouds darkened the horizon; the wind moaned among the trees, and rustled the willows that fringed the river. Fleurette felt frightened; a foreboding of evil weighed upon her, and she looked timidly at her companion, whose morose expression did not relieve her fears. She cheered herself with the thought, however, that they were returning home, and the storm would not break out until they had reached the village. But before Bernard had rowed many yards, he abruptly snatched the rudder lines, and, suddenly leaving the main channel of the river, forced his little craft up a narrow stream to the right.

" Where are you going ? Surely this is not the way home ? " said Fleurette, pale with alarm, and shivering perceptibly. " I have not even my cloak with me, and I shall get drenched if the rain comes down."

" The rain will come down in less than five minutes, and you may prepare yourself for a wetting ; but there is a cottage on the left bank, a little higher up, where we can take shelter until the storm is over.

It would be hopeless to try and reach the village."

Bernard had stopped rowing ; but, with the help of the oar, was pushing the boat through the rushes, which were so rank that it was almost impossible to proceed. Nothing could exceed the wildness and gloomy desolation of the scene around. The thick bank of clouds cast their shadows upon the flat, bare landscape, whose monotony was solely relieved by a few stunted poplars. The wild birds broke the silence now and then by a discordant screech, as the bow of the boat disturbed the dank willows in which they had taken temporary refuge.

"We must land here," said Bernard, pushing the boat as close as he could to the bank. "The cottage ought to be somewhere hereabouts, although I don't see it; but we shall find it as soon as we get out."

"Oh, let us go home! It is getting very late, and Miss Bouverie will think something has happened to us. We should have been half-way home by this, if you had not come among these horrid rushes. Do get in, and let us return," urged Fleurette, in a piteous tone of voice.

But Bernard turned a deaf ear to her entreaties. He had jumped out on the bank, and was dragging the boat closer to the shore, while she as persistently clung to the far side, and refused to leave it.

While the struggle was going on between them, a boat, which had hitherto been concealed among the rushes, glided alongside, and Fleurette, hearing a well known voice, looked round, and recognized Donald Stamer. With a sudden bound, she sprang to her feet, almost capsizing the frail craft in her eagerness to reach him.

"You have just come in time, Stamer," said Bernard, with amazing *sang-froid*. "These confounded weeds have completely stopped our progress, and Fleurette has no muffling with her. I am glad to see that you have brought a cloak for her."

"It seems to me that you are doing your best to overturn the boat, and I may congratulate Miss de Ruthvyn on her narrow escape," rejoined Donald, stiffly. "If you will permit me," added he, addressing Fleurette, "I will row you back." As he spoke, he lifted the trembling girl from the one boat to the other, and wrapped a warm cloak round her. "I shall not waste time discussing the matter with you now, Bernard," con-

tinued Donald, "but by-and-by I shall
call you to account for endangering Miss
de Ruthvyn's life. In the mean time, you
had better get some one to assist you
with the boat, or it will very soon go to
the bottom."

Bernard gave an angry rejoinder from
the bank, while his friend rowed away.
Not a word passed between Fleurette and
her companion for upwards of half a mile.
She ventured at length to look at him,
but his face was as pale as her own, and
the sternness of his look unnerved her.
Her tears began to flow, and a sob now
and then was heard, in spite of her efforts
to conceal it.

"It distresses me to see you weep,"
said Donald, after a few moments. "No
doubt, you are angry with me for taking
you from Bernard, but it will be all well
to-morrow. There is nothing that I

know of to prevent you from being engaged to one another. You may meet as often as ever you like ; but don't let us have the scandal of an elopement."

Fleurette flashed an indignant glance at Donald through her tears. " How dare you accuse me of such a thing ? " said she, quivering with passion. " How dare you say that I wanted to elope with Bernard Waldstein—I, who hate him, who would rather die fifty deaths than marry him ? " and, unable to repress her grief any longer, she burst into hysterical sobs, burying her face in her hands.

" How glad I am to hear you say this, Fleurette ! I don't like Bernard myself, and should be sorry to see you married to him, but you cannot blame me for my mistake. I knew he loved you, and I could not fail to notice the encouragement you gave him. Why did you go with him to-day, when I asked you as a favour not to do so?" Donald's voice had assumed a very tender tone, and, leaning forward, he tried to take her hands from her face.

"I did it because—because," sobbed Fleurette, "you seemed not to care for me."

"Not care!" echoed Donald, a glad flush of surprise rising to his face. "I care very much for you, Fleurette; perhaps too much, if the truth were told. Your interests have been very dear to me ever since I met you years ago at Delamere. You must tell me all about Bernard now, that I may know how to act, for he must leave Driancourt to-morrow."

"It is I who should leave," interrupted Fleurette. "Bernard asked me to marry him the first day he arrived, and made me promise afterwards that I would not tell any one. I did not like to break my word, though I often wished to tell Miss Bouverie, as it was so unpleasant for me. I would have gone away myself, but I could not forego the pleasure of being with you."

"And I drove you from me to-day, when you asked me to stay with you. Can you ever forgive me, Fleurette?" said her companion, taking her slender hand in his, and kissing it.

Fleurette was too happy to speak. Who could have foretold that the day would have had so blissful an ending? What had she further to fear? What doubts, what misunderstandings, could separate her from the man she loved? All the wretchedness of uncertainty was over, and before her stretched a future of delight.

And what were Donald's thoughts? He had not sought Fleurette s love. It was an unlooked-for gift, which he had unexpectedly discovered; but he did not the less appreciate it. It was a consolation, after all the bitter disappointments of life, to find that he had won the heart of one so fair and lovable. He could not accept her love, he knew. There was the painful task before him of undeceiving her; but he would not tell her anything to grieve her to-night. She had suffered enough already, and he would let her have this short hour of happiness. So he listened to her sweet voice, felt the warm clasp of her hand, and put away the thoughts of the future.

All traces of the storm had passed away, and the gentle plashing of the oars was the only sound that broke the stillness of the scene. The moon rose

from behind a bank of clouds, and shed
its silvery light upon the wanderers,
while an occasional star twinkled in the
high arch of heaven.

CHAPTER XII.

THE following morning, Bernard relieved
Colonel Stamer from the disagreeable
duty of giving him his *congé*, by saying
at breakfast that he had received a letter
which would oblige him to return to
London at once. He was partly reconciled to the necessity of leaving Driancourt by the thought that Fleurette
would no longer keep his proposal a
secret. He knew, too, that he would
find it difficult to exculpate his conduct
to his host and hostess; and that, even
should he succeed in putting a favourable
construction on it, and be permitted to

remain, he would be too closely watched
in the future to effect his purpose. He
was not drawing upon his imagination
altogether when he said that he had received an important letter, as a very
surprising one, to say the least of it, had
reached him from his sister the day
before. It had been following him about
from town to town, as appeared from
the envelope covered with postmarks,
and had been forwarded to Driancourt.
from the Hotel de Russie. In this letter
Evelyn showed that she wished to be
reconciled to him, and invited him to
spend the autumn with her in Scotland.
She concluded by saying that she had
been greatly annoyed by a false report
which had been circulated lately, announcing her engagement to Lord Ilberry.
She begged Bernard to contradict it upon
every possible opportunity, as there was

no foundation for it. She would never
marry again, she asserted; she had quite
made up her mind upon that subject.
There would be a wedding before very
long at Delamere, she hoped, but it
would be Raymond's, and not her own.
He was engaged to Fleurette, and they
would be married as soon as he came of
age, and then the dearest wish of her
heart would be fulfilled.

This letter, instead of conciliating Bernard, had the effect of rousing his worst
feelings. He had been but little troubled
at what Fleurette had said about her
engagement to Raymond, as her words
conclusively showed that she did not
regard it as binding on her cousin or herself; but it was evident to him now that
Evelyn had set her heart upon it. It
would be a quietus to her conscience,
no doubt, and he very much feared that

Fleurette would be no match for her. She would have to yield to her persuasions when she was back in England, and Raymond might insist on her return at any moment. Exasperated at this new aspect of affairs, Bernard was all the more savage with Donald Stamer for coming between him and Fleurette the evening before. Only for his unwarrantable interference, all would have gone well. Before setting out on the boating-excursion, he had fully made up his mind to arrange matters in such a way that Fleurette should believe she had compromised herself. It was, as he knew, the only way that he could induce her to marry him. He had the whole plan sketched out before starting, and the very elements had conspired in his favour. The storm had given him a good excuse for urging Fleurette to land,

and, if she had yielded, she would have been compelled to spend the night in some lonely cottage, as he would have taken care to send the boat adrift. It would have been easy afterwards to make her believe that she had hopelessly offended Miss Bouverie, and there would have been no option left her but to marry him. It was to Donald that he owed the complete discomfiture of his scheme, and he was so enraged with him that he could not deny himself the pleasure of giving him a parting thrust as he was about to leave Driancourt.

"Any message for Evelyn?" he said, in as careless a tone as he could assume, while his portmanteau was being placed in the tax-cart which Colonel Stamer was lending to expedite his departure ·from Driancourt. "I expect to be at Monkhurst in a few days, and to hear all about the approaching marriages. Evelyn's is to come off first, and Raymond's afterwards. You have heard, no doubt, about Lord Ilberry?"

Donald had heard about Lord Ilberry, and the subject was evidently unpleasant to him.

"He may thank his interference for that disagreeable piece of news," Bernard soliloquized, as he drove down the avenue, uncertain whether he would return to England at once, or take the chance of seeing Fleurette again by remaining at Brussels. His chances of success seemed small, but he was resolved not to throw up the game yet.

Fleurette, meanwhile, was sitting at the open window of her bedroom, and had not yet made her appearance for the day downstairs. She had lain in a half-waking, half-sleeping state for some hours before rising; and, though now dressed and sitting in an arm-chair, with the light breeze from the garden fanning her cheeks, she found such pleasant companionship in her own thoughts, that she was not inclined to disturb herself. She was thinking of her moonlight row on the river, and recalling every look and word of Donald Stamer's. No doubt, he was waiting for her impatiently downstairs, she thought, but she felt a wonderful shyness at meeting him.

She was aroused from her reverie presently by seeing Miss Bouverie walking in the direction of the aviary, and, looking at her watch, was startled to perceive that it was nearly twelve o'clock. Since her arrival at Driancourt, she usually attended to the birds at this hour, and she felt a sudden remorse at having forgotten them.

Finishing her toilet as rapidly as possible, she went downstairs, and, crossing the hall, noticed a couple of portmanteaus, which she concluded were Bernard's. She had heard from the servant that he had left, but she took for granted that he had given directions for his luggage to be sent after him. On reaching the lawn, she looked in vain for Miss Bouverie. The aviary doors were locked. There was no one in the greenhouse but the gardener, and she was about to return to the house, when she saw Donald Stamer approaching her. Fleurette looked very pretty in her pale blue cashmere gown, with the May sun shining upon her golden hair; but, though she had been expecting to meet Donald, a timid expression stole over her face as he came towards her.

"I have been looking for you everywhere, and could not think where you were hiding," said he. " Will you come into the library, as I want to talk to you, and the sun is so hot here that it will spoil your complexion ? "

Donald spoke cheerfully, but Fleurette thought his tone and manner were constrained, and a vague fear came over her as she accompanied him indoors. Her alarm increased when she stood face to face with him in the library, and noticed his white, agitated looks. She remained standing, though he sat down and tried to make her sit beside him.

" What is the matter ? Something terrible must have happened ! " she exclaimed, in a breathless tone.

" Nothing, Fleurette, except that I must say good-bye to you, as I am obliged to leave Driancourt to-day."

" But you will come back again to-

morrow, or in a few days," she added,
her heart beating so violently that she
could scarcely speak.

"I don't think so. My movements
must be uncertain for a time. Won't
you believe that I am sorry, very sorry,
at having to leave?" he continued, looking anxiously at the terrible whiteness
which was stealing over her face.

"Why must you go away?" she
faltered, in a timid, despairing voice, as
though she shrank from hearing the
answer.

"It is difficult to tell you why, my
child. It would be a long story, and
would only pain your sensitive nature.
I have said hard things of Bernard, and
he deserved them; but I should be a
hundred times more culpable than he if
I remained. Honour and duty both
oblige me to go, dearest Fleurette,

though inclination would bid me stay. Some day, when you are older, perhaps when you are married, I shall tell you the history of my life. It has not been a happy one, and the consciousness that I have brought pain and grief to you is another sorrow added to the long list of what I have already had to bear. Will you not tell me that you forgive me?" he continued, as he placed his arm round her and endeavoured to draw her towards him.

"What do you wish me to say?" cried Fleurette, in a tone of intense bitterness, turning round her pain-stricken countenance, which she had hitherto kept averted. "I will do or say anything you wish, if you unsay your cruel words—if you tell me that you will not leave me."

"You must not tempt me to stay, Fleurette. At the risk of incurring your hatred, I must leave you, but you will not hate me; you will only forget me. The sorrows of the young do not last long. You will soon forget the passing fancy you have taken for a man old enough to be your father, and you will have ceased to think of him long before he forgets you. Comfort yourself with the thought, my very dearest child, if it be any comfort to you, that in the hours spent in your company I have had the nearest approach to happiness which I have known for years. In days to come, I shall picture you to myself, matured, yet lovelier than ever, the centre of a happy and honoured home, and then I shall rejoice that I overcame to-day. My own unhappiness is of small account. My life has been one long mistake, and I have struggled through a greater sorrow than this already."

As Colonel Stamer spoke, the recollection of that former sorrow swept over
him, and he trembled and became white
with emotion.   Then, not daring to pro-
long a scene which had already unnerved
him, he pressed a kiss upon Fleurette's
forehead, and hurried out of the room.

CHAPTER XIII.

THOUGH Fleurette had not mentioned Bernard's proposal to Miss Bouverie, she had not been so silent on the subject to Teresa. She had written a long letter to the Italian girl, the very day after Bernard's arrival at Driancourt, chaffing her about her wonderful spirit of prophecy, and telling her that what she had foretold about Mr. Waldstein, unlikely as it had seemed to her at the time, had literally come to pass. Fleurette wrote in the innocence of her heart, little dreaming what effect her letter would have upon the vindictive and fiery-tempered Teresa. She guessed that the girl had taken some dislike to Bernard, but thought it mere caprice, and knew nothing whatever about his bad treatment of her. Teresa could have forgiven Bernard for not marrying her if she could believe that he had ever loved her genuinely, but since Monsieur Dufour had opened her eyes to the fact that it was Fleurette and her money he had wanted, and that he had shammed love for herself merely to secure the benefit of her services, she had conceived the most intense hatred towards him. Fleurette's letter confirmed her worst suspicions of him, but had a fortunate influence on her so far as Monsieur Dufour was concerned, as, ten days after she received it, she met him at Dieppe, and was married to him in the church of St. Jacques. Before joining herself in the bonds of matrimony with the fond and faithful Frenchman, she made him promise to assist her in punishing her perfidious lover.

Monsieur Dufour was not at all reluctant to give the promise. He disliked Bernard almost as heartily as Teresa did, and was determined to save Fleurette from him, if for no other reason than that she was the daughter of his beloved master, Philip de Ruthvyn. He prided himself upon his cleverness, but, clever as he was, he was dull compared with Teresa, the natural bent of whose mind was intrigue. She was not many days married, when she made her husband write a letter at her dictation to Bernard, which she posted to the Hotel de Russie, and which reached him there about ten days after his return from Driancourt. Bernard's spirits were at the lowest ebb at this time. He had not once seen Fleurette since the memorable

evening of their boating adventure, and
had no opportunity of exculpating himself
to her. He was uneasy, too, about the
papers, and feared that Monsieur Dufour
had already parted with them, either to
Evelyn or Fleurette herself. He had
written to him twice about them within
the last six months, and had tried to
come to terms, but had received no
reply. He was thinking seriously of
going to Rouen, and of offering the hotel-
keeper his own price for them, when the
letter reached him. It was a letter
which puzzled him a good deal at first,
and he read it with feelings of distrust,
though he little suspected Teresa had
any hand in it.

Monsieur Dufour commenced by apolo-
gizing for not having answered his letters
sooner. He had lately been married,
and Monsieur Waldstein, he felt sure,

would excuse him under the circumstances for apparent negligence. His
wife, strange to say, was quite in the
confidence of the young lady in whom
monsieur was so deeply interested, and
knew all about the love-affair that was
going on between them. Why, continued
the Frenchman, had not Monsieur Waldstein been thoroughly confidential with
him ? Perhaps it was because he feared
he was not a successful lover. He was
not to be down-hearted. The young lady
had refused him once, but was by no
means inclined to reject him finally.
Madame Dufour had extraordinary influence with her, and was willing to use
that influence in favour of her husband's
client. With regard to the papers, he
had them still in his possession, and
would forward them to Monsieur Waldstein on receipt of nine hundred francs.

Bernard thought a good deal over this letter, and suspected there was something at the bottom of Madame Dufour's offer of assistance. Who was she? Where had the Frenchman met her, and in what way had she come across Fleurette? Her co-operation would be worth something, if she could bring about an interview between him and the latter; but he was determined to be on his guard. He saw that Dufour had come down in his price for the papers just as he had expected, and congratulated himself upon having delayed his offer. He was resolved not to part with the money until the documents were placed in his hand, and was about to write to that effect, when a second letter reached him from the Frenchman, telling him that he would be in Brussels in a few weeks, and that he would call to see him at the Hotel de Russie.

One sultry afternoon in July, about six weeks after Monsieur Dufour had posted his second letter to Bernard, he and Teresa were enjoying their *café noir* in a private sitting-room of the Lévrier, the principal inn of Louvain. They had matters to discuss which necessitated a room to themselves, but as a rule they both liked society, and Monsieur Dufour was still a great favourite with the fair sex. Many an admiring glance was bestowed upon him during the period of his bachelorhood at Rouen, and many hopes were dashed to the ground when he announced his marriage and Teresa suddenly appeared as presiding mistress of his establishment. The latter was looking unusually well. The exciting nature of the topic she was discussing had brought a flush to her cheeks, and her eyes sparkled with unusual brilliancy.

Some letters written in French lay upon the table near her, which she seemed to be studying eagerly, while she referred every now and then to her husband at any portion of them that was unintelligible to her.

" *Cara mia*, but you are in a state of excitement," said Monsieur Dufour. " Give me another cup of coffee, and try to compose your nerves. Is it the sight of your former lover's handwriting that has brought that becoming flush to your cheeks ? You have not looked so young and so handsome since you did me the honour of becoming Madame Dufour."

Teresa frowned, and looked contemptuously at her husband. "I am in no humour for joking, Paul. I have an old score to settle with this former lover of mine, and I won't sleep to-night until I arrange how to pay it off."

" Fortune seems to befriend you, *chère amie*. Whom do you think I saw on the steps of the Hotel de Suède about an hour ago ? "

" Not Monsieur Waldstein? " ejaculated Teresa.

" No; but one who would be a very good match for him. You remember Colonel Stamer, who left Brussels two months ago ? "

" Yes. But what about him? I don't see how he is to help us."

" He is here in this town, not three streets off. My advice would be to take him into our confidence, and to tell him how Mr. Waldstein is scheming to entrap the poor young girl into a marriage."

"Not for worlds!" cried Teresa, starting up with such vehemence that she overturned the coffee-cup, and spilled the contents. " Don't attempt to mention

Miss de Ruthvyn's name to him. I won't have a stranger dragged in to meddle with my affairs. Leave Monsieur Waldstein and his schemes to me." The Italian woman spoke with breathless rapidity, and her features worked with a convulsive tremor.

Monsieur Dufour looked on admiringly. "*Morbleu!* You would make our fortune on the stage. Such fire! such grace! Your pose is perfection. You would make an admirable Lady Macbeth. I knew, the night I went with you to the Lyceum in London, that you had a genius for the drama."

"Can you not be serious, Paul? I have told you already that I am in no humour for empty compliments. If you will listen to my directions, it will be a great deal more to the purpose."

While Teresa was speaking, a blinding

flash of lightning, followed by a loud peal
of thunder, caused her to start away from
the open window, near which she had
been sitting.

"We are in for a wild night," said
Paul, looking out of the window, while
the river that rolled beneath was revealed
by a second and more vivid flash. "I
had better fasten the shutters before you
take me into your confidence about this
wonderful plot of yours."

The rain was descending in torrents,
and Teresa's thoughts were for a moment
diverted from Bernard Waldstein, while
she looked out at the lurid flashes that
every now and then lit up the pitchy
blackness of the sky.

"It makes one shudder to look at that
whirling river," said she. "Shut it out
from sight, Paul, and let us go on with
our business."

Monsieur Dufour did as he was directed. He rang for an additional lamp, securely fastened the windows and persiennes, and succeeded in giving a more comfortable appearance to the room.

" Do not think that I am anxious to save Monsieur Waldstein," said he, as Teresa was about to recommence her argument. "I have no reason to screen that slippery gentleman. He would have cheated me under my very nose of the sum he agreed to pay me, only I proved a match for him. We go full shares in our prejudices against him, *chère amie;* but for all that, we may as well act so as to benefit ourselves ultimately. Now, this Colonel Stamer is a friend of Mademoiselle Fleurette, and for aught we know may be an admirer of hers. She has been staying often at his aunt's house. He could balk Mr. Waldstein of his prize in the most effectual manner by carrying her off himself, and if we placed the proofs of her parentage in his hand, he and she would no doubt agree to pay us well for our pains."

"You are thinking of money, Paul. My thoughts are above paltry greed. I am thinking of how I will best pay off Mr. Bernard Waldstein for his dastardly conduct to myself, and if you make an ally of Colonel Stamer, he will entirely upset my plans. What is Miss de Ruthvyn to me, that I should hesitate to make a dupe of her to secure my own aims? But do you think Colonel Stamer would allow me to do so? It is likely enough that he will marry her, but it concerns us very little whether he does or not. If we tell him all we know about her parentage, he will probably pay us for our information; but that would be small

satisfaction to me. Bernard Waldstein
must be punished, and must be met with
treachery equal to his own; and I tell
you, Paul, my plans are already succeeding
beyond my expectation. See the dear,
loving little note, that in his innocent
simplicity he entrusts to me to forward
to Miss de Ruthvyn," continued she, in a
bitter tone of voice, while she unfolded a
letter, which she glanced at contemptuously, and then tore into shreds. " I
am looking forward with glee to writing
the reply. It shall be quite as loving as
his own, and he shall never doubt but
that it comes from the heiress. See by
this letter of his, too, how he leaves
everything in our hands. He trusts to
woman's wit, he says, to overcome all
obstacles, and counts upon finding Miss
de Ruthvyn in a more loving mood when
next he meets her. Little he thinks that

the trusted ally, who is to be his stepping-
stone to fortune, is his despised tool, the
woman whom he befooled and jilted, but
who will prove more than a match for
him yet."

"You will get yourself into a scrape,
my dear girl, if you allow your passions
to get the mastery over you. Don't
think of Bernard any more. He is too
contemptible to waste such an amount of
feeling on."

"Have no fear for me, Paul; I am not
going to endanger my life, or peril my
soul, which is worse, for a thing like this.
No serious harm shall happen him, I
promise you; but I have sworn that he
shall be paid back in his own coin. You
see by his last letter that he leaves it to
us to engage the clergyman. I have
even made arrangements for the house
where he is to spend the honeymoon.

You know the damp, lonely looking building which we noticed the day we were at La Roche? It is there I propose driving my gallant friend, Mr. Waldstein, and I hope he may enjoy his honeymoon. You must write to-morrow, and appoint to meet him at the *Cerf noir;* but you must let me know the precise hour and day he chooses for the rendezvous. You must tell him that Mademoiselle Fleurette consents to the clandestine marriage, and that she will arrive at Rixensart, accompanied by your wife, a short time after himself. No doubt, he will be watching for her, which will suit my purpose very well, as he will feel all the more certain of her if he sees her arriving. You must tell him, however, that she wishes to rest in the inn, and that, to avoid all scandal, she will remain in her own room until the appointed hour when she is to

take her place in the carriage beside
him."

"Do you really mean that Miss de
Ruthvyn is to accompany Mr. Waldstein
to the house you have hired?" said Paul,
with a look of anger.

"How thick-headed you are!" replied
Teresa, pettishly. "Did I not tell you
that I was bent upon making a fool of
him? Mademoiselle Fleurette's journey
ends at the little inn at Rixensart. It is
I, Teresa Dufour, whom he will find
seated in the carriage, and who will drive
with him to the house I have hired. We
won't mind stopping at the church on the
way, as there won't be need for the cere-
mony." Teresa leaned back in her chair,
and indulged in a hearty fit of laughter,
while Monsieur looked at her in bewilder-
ment. "You need not look so puzzled,
mon ami," continued she, still laughing.

"It will be much easier to manage than you think, and you need not fear that I am going to run away with our dear friend, Monsieur Waldstein. I am only going to act a little comedy for his especial benefit. I am much the same height as Mademoiselle, and I have ordered a hat and travelling-cloak precisely such as she wears, which I shall have conveyed to the inn the day before. Your sister Madelon is thoroughly interested in the affair, and will keep Mademoiselle Fleurette in conversation while I adopt the disguise. Her brother-in-law from Brussels is providing the carriage, and is to be coachman on the occasion, and his nephew André is to be footman. They will both have firearms, so, you see, I shall be well protected."

"Silly girl!" interrupted Monsieur Dufour; "your fun will be of short duration. Monsieur Waldstein will not be five minutes sitting beside you, when he will discover you are not the lady he wants."

" I am not so sure of that," replied Teresa, in a piqued tone of voice; "among my other accomplishments, I can mimic a voice to perfection, and he is so accustomed to the constrained and frigid manner of Mademoiselle Fleurette, that he will not wonder at her being a little silent on such an occasion. If I am not greatly mistaken, he will be so over-joyed at his good luck, that he will trouble himself very little about the humour of his lady-love."

" He will think she is in an unusually shy mood, eh ? " said Paul, with a know-ing look.

" If the worst comes to the worst, and that he discovers his mistake," continued

Teresa, ignoring her husband's last remark; "I shall exchange my seat inside for one beside my friend Mathieu, on the box. He and André will pinion the gallant bridegroom if he becomes restive, and will let him have a scent of the gunpowder. He will be quiet enough after that, I imagine."

"Hush!" said Paul, interrupting her, and walking over towards the window. "Do you not hear a bell? I have noticed it at intervals during the last quarter of an hour."

"I hear nothing but the rain," replied Teresa, in a sulky tone, aggrieved that her husband's thoughts should be occupied with anything but herself and her affairs.

Monsieur Dufour, in the mean time, unfastened the shutters, and was peering out of the window, when the booming sound of an alarm-bell vibrated upon the air.

"Do you not hear that now?" continued he. "The storm must have done some serious damage."

"It is far more likely to be a fire somewhere in the town. Let us go into the coffee-room and inquire. They will know all about it there," rejoined Teresa.

The room in which Madame Dufour and her husband had been conversing was in the back of the inn. They had to descend a portion of the staircase, and cross a corridor to reach the coffee-room. On their way they were met by a waiter, who enlightened them about the bell.

Madame was right; it was a fire, but it was some distance off, he told them. It was a lunatic asylum, about a mile up the river. Some people said it had been struck by lightning, others that one of the inmates had escaped, and had set it on fire. The glow of the flames could be distinctly seen from the top window. All the gentlemen in the hotel had gone to see it, although the rain was still coming down pretty smartly.

" The rain won't keep me in, either. Who knows what assistance I may be able to give to those unfortunate creatures?" said Monsieur Dufour, not venturing to look at Teresa, who bridled up at once at the notion of his departure. She knew, however, that it was vain to oppose him, as, with all his cajoleries and pleasant manners, Monsieur Dufour had a very firm will of his own. She contented herself, therefore, with injunctions not to approach too close to the burning building, and to keep at a still safer distance from the lunatics; and, having satisfied herself that the worst of the

storm was over, and that Paul had his
overcoat and umbrella, she sat down to
peruse *Galignani* in the deserted coffee-
room, while Monsieur Dufour bargained
with a boatman to row him to the scene
of the fire.

END OF VOL. II.

LONDON: PRINTED BY WILLIAM CLOWES AND SONS, LIMITED,
STAMFORD STREET AND CHARING CROSS.

www.ingramcontent.com/pod-product-compliance
Lightning Source LLC
Chambersburg PA
CBHW022000050726
47498CB00006BA/2191